HER DIRTY BARTENDERS: A SECOND CHANCE ROMANCE

A MEN AT WORK REVERSE HAREM NOVEL

MIKA LANE

HEADLANDS PUBLISHING

COPYRIGHT

BE THE FIRST TO KNOW...

Want more heat, heart,
and bad boys who know what they're doing?
Join my list and I'll send the steam straight to your inbox,
starting with a deliciously naughty story:

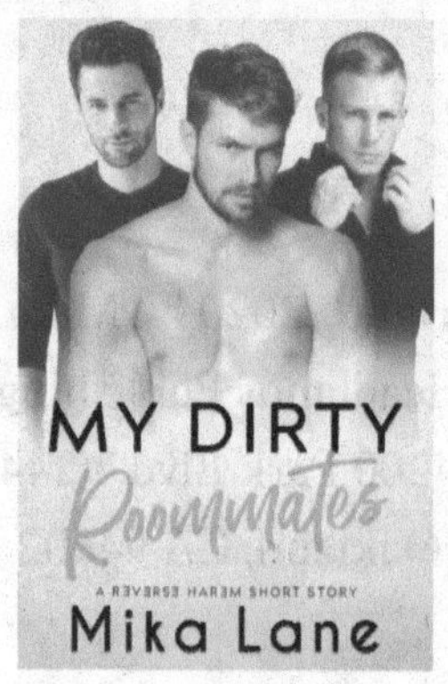

SIGN UP TO MY MAILING LIST!
Or visit:
https://geni.us/free-book-signup

Estella "Stell" Kline

"LICENSE AND REGISTRATION PLEASE, MA'AM."

Shit.

"Here you go, Officer," I said with my best *this doesn't suck* smile.

Fingers crossed he wouldn't notice my registration was a bit... out of date. If he did, I was really screwed.

The state trooper, or highway patrol, or whatever it was they had in the state of Colorado, strolled back to his car, where he'd left the lights flashing for the enjoyment of every rubbernecker driving by, and settled in to do whatever they do with your identification.

I turned the volume back up on my Beyoncé station, and rested my head against the steering wheel.

I'd been driving a good eight hours. Time for a break. Except this wasn't the sort of break I'd planned on.

And getting rear-ended in traffic had also not been part of my plan.

Particularly not by a sports-car-driving douchebag who couldn't be bothered to apologize for plowing into the back of my Toyota Corolla. I supposed he felt my car wasn't worth apologizing over, but dammit, it was the only car I had.

And it was the one that was supposed to take me from Philadelphia all the way to Los Angeles, where I was going to Start a New Life. One without the baggage of being a congressman's daughter, and one out of the eye of the paparazzi always waiting for me to fuck up.

And one really far away from the asshole fiancé I'd just bailed on.

I squinted at the glare of the blinding cop car lights. "Marni!" I said to my BFF when she picked up on the first ring.

By my estimation, I was only fifteen minutes from her place. Didn't it just figure that, in the last fifteen minutes of a long-ass and seriously boring drive, I'd get in a car accident.

"Stell! Heya, sweetie, are you close? I got the margarita fixings ready to roll—"

Out of the corner of my eye, Douchebag paced, looking back and forth between the damage to his car, and then mine.

It was clear to me he was going to be responsible for this mess, so he *should* be upset. Dude was going to end up spending some money paying for repairs on *two* cars.

Actually, *I* was upset too. I'd thought I could slip by with expired tags until I had the money to re-register them. But I had a feeling I was about to be called out.

"I just got in a fender bender," I blurted, interrupting Marni's margarita run-down.

She gasped. "OH MY GOD. Are you okay?"

I pictured her face creased with concern, her short, black Cleopatra-style hair bouncing around her face.

"I'm totally fine, Marn. I just have to wait for the state trooper to do his bit. I already got the insurance info from the asshole who hit me."

I heard her rushing around in the background, keys jangling. "I'm coming right now. Tell me exactly where you are," she cried as if I were bleeding to death, missing a limb, or needing the Jaws of Life.

"No, no, no. It's not that serious. The back of my car is bashed in, but fortunately I can still drive. I'll be there as soon as I can."

"Oh sweetie, that sucks. It just sucks. This was supposed to be a celebration of your arrival in Denver, dammit."

I hope this wasn't an indication of what was to come.

"Girl, I'm gonna need to celebrate more than ever, now," I said. "Put that booze on ice. I'll be there soon."

The state trooper walked back up to my car.

"You're a long way from Pennsylvania, Ms. Kline," he said.

I nodded, stopping just short of telling him the details of my life plans. "Yes. I'm on my way to LA. Stopping in Denver for a few days to visit my BFF."

His left eyebrow rose.

He didn't know what BFF was.

"I see. Cross country road trip. So, Ms. Kline, can you step out of the car?"

I looked out my open window at him. He was cute as hell but practicing quite the mean face.

"Oh. Sure, Officer. Should I, um, turn my car off? Or just keep it running?"

What was the etiquette in situations like this?

He nodded. "Turn it off, please."

I popped out of the car, smoothing out my miniskirt, but making sure it swung just right as I approached not only the trooper, but also the jerk who had rammed my car.

I crossed my arms because that's what they were both doing. And furrowed my brow to look more serious.

"Here's your ID back, Ms. Kline. Here's yours, Mr. Stryker. Since there are no injuries, and you've exchanged insurance information, you are free to go." He looked directly at Douchebag.

"Thank you, Officer," Douchebag said, extending a hand for a shake.

Suck up.

"Before you go, Mr. Stryker, I just wanted to say that although you were the one to hit Ms. Kline's car"—he looked at me for emphasis—"if she'd been paying better attention and not come to a quick stop, none of this would have happened."

What? Did he really just say that?

Smug worked itself across Douchebag's face.

I don't think so.

I turned to him. "Smile all you want, because you're the one who's going to pay for all this damage to my car." The last few words slipped out loudly. Like, *yelling* loudly.

I stormed back to my car. I was calling his insurance company first thing in the morning. That fucker wouldn't have a moment of peace until they cut me a check to get my car fixed.

"Ms. Kline, I'm not through with you yet," the trooper called after me.

Crap.

Douchebag stood there, nosy as the rubberneckers slowing traffic, clearly hoping to get some satisfaction about any further misfortune coming my way.

"Your car registration is expired."

Truer words were never spoken.

"Oh, that's right," I said, dramatically smacking my forehead. "Shoot. I forgot to send the check for the renewal before I left town. I'll do it first thing, tomorrow," I lied.

With all the shit going on in my life, the worst of it was that I was dead broke. There was no way in hell I paying for my registration renewal tomorrow. Or the next day. I needed all the money I had just to get to LA.

"Ms. Kline, the penalty for expired tags is pretty hefty."

I nodded. "I know, Officer," I said, hoping my platform sandals were elongating my legs to maximum effect.

He handed me the top piece of paper from his notebook. I was hoping it might be his number.

It was not.

In fact, it was a ticket.

Fuuuuuck.

I folded it neatly in half, planning to look at the fine later, at Marni's, after I'd had a margarita or two.

I smiled stiffly as Douchebag enjoyed my pain. "Is that everything?" I asked.

He nodded politely. "Yes. You may go now. Please drive more carefully. Both of you."

I trudged back to my car, the officer and douchebag continuing to chat like they were buds. And just as I got my opening in traffic, I rolled down my window.

"Hey, guys."

They looked over at me.

"Go fuck yourselves!" I screamed, and hit the road.

____

2

Stell

"MARN, THIS APARTMENT TOTALLY ROCKS," I said, wandering around and trying not to drool.

Of course she had a gorgeous place. Marni had always had nice things, thanks to a nice jumpstart known as her dad's massive fortune.

She looked around, nodding. "Thank you Stell. I really love it. It's so homey… and just totally *me*."

She was right. Her place was totally her, with its white overstuffed sofa and chairs, and vases of pink roses all over.

But it was all good. Marni was about the most down-to-earth person I'd ever known, and she deserved all good things that came her way.

The moment I dropped my things in the guestroom she'd shown me to—where I had my own bathroom!—I pulled on my PJs and joined her in the living room.

"You're finally here," she said, raising a glass after she'd poured two of her excellent margaritas. "Cheers to changing shit up."

That was about the most tactful way I'd heard my latest fuck-up referred to.

"And how is the sad and broken hearted Vaughn Breslin?" she asked. "The erstwhile groom?"

Ugh. I hated the sound of that man's name. But her questions were legit. She'd known him a long time, just like I had.

I pushed around a pile of Vanity Fair magazines, perfectly styled on Marni's coffee table, with my toe.

"Not sure. He hates being alone, so I suppose he'll run back to some old girlfriend until he gets his sea legs back and is ready to find a new woman. And then he can cheat on her, too."

Marni looked into her margarita, shaking her head. "Crazy shit, cancelling a wedding at the last minute. But I applaud you for it. Takes a lot of balls."

She wasn't kidding.

"Hey, I think my mom is shipping back your wedding present," I offered.

She wrinkled her nose. "Oh just keep it. It was a serving platter from Tiffany. I'm sure you'll use it."

Holy shit. I hadn't realized that. I made a mental note to tell Mom to set that one aside.

Mom was all about etiquette. Even though she was clearly mortified by my calling off my wedding at the last minute, she dutifully called each guest, apologized, and ensured them that their gifts would be returned.

"So, let's go outside. I want to see what happened to your car," she said, standing.

I wrinkled my nose. "We're in our pajamas."

She shrugged. "Nobody here cares. Plus, I'm friends with most everyone in the complex. So, c'mon."

I followed her outside to the guest parking spot she'd directed me to, and got a lump in my throat when I looked at my poor car.

Something white caught my eye and I peered in the window at the registration citation I'd forgotten. I opened the car and tried to snatch it before Marni saw it. She already felt sorry enough for me.

"You got a ticket, too?"

I tried to hide my crumpling face in the dim light of the parking lot, and I might have if a stifled sob hadn't given me away.

"Oh, sweetie," Marni said, rubbing my arm. "Let's go back inside. You'll feel better soon. You've had a lot going on. First, Vaughn, now this."

"But… you don't… under… stand," I wailed.

She slung an arm around my shoulders. "What? What don't I understand?"

I buried my face in my hands as the tears flowed. "I… I don't know how… I'll get to LA now. This car repair is going to take the last of my… money."

I figured insurance would pay for the repairs, but who knew how long that sort of thing took. I'd probably have to pay up front to get the car fixed.

"Every... thing... is so... fucked up," I sniffled.

"Okay. Let's get back inside."

She led me like the pathetic thing I was.

She sat me down in her living room, and paced the floor in front of me. "You'll stay in Denver with me while you get back on your feet. Stay as long as you want."

My mother had always said fish and company started to stink after three days.

I didn't want to stink. I loved my friendship with Marni way too much for that.

"Maybe you can find some temporary work here, and earn a little money before you move on."

Ugh. Doing what? I'd just left my short-lived profession as a kindergarten teacher. I didn't mind the kids, but I felt like more of a babysitter than a teacher. And then there were the dads who always hit on me.

I had big plans for LA. I was going to become a yoga instructor and live on the beach. I'd probably see celebrities all the time, and eat gobs of good sushi.

At least that was the plan. But instead, here I was, stuck halfway across the country.

Her generosity moved me, regardless. "Thank you, Marn. That's so generous. But I don't know."

She threw her hands in the air. "What's not to

know? You'll stay here until you have a little money saved, and then continue on your journey."

I looked up to find her wearing her 'case closed' expression.

The problem was, I didn't want to stay in Denver any longer than I had to. It seemed nice and all, except for the fender bender and ticket I'd gotten the moment I arrived in the city limits, but I wanted palm trees and sunshine. And white sandy beaches.

That was my plan. Hanging out in Denver was not. And no one loved a good plan more than I did.

But maybe I shouldn't rush to judgment. The truth was, I didn't know a damn thing about Denver, except that my best friend from childhood, Marni, lived there.

It was the first time I'd seen her in probably three—or was it four—years? Her trips to Philly, our hometown, had become less and less frequent over time thanks to the demands of her difficult father and disinterested mother.

"Just sleep on it, okay?" she asked sweetly.

God, if I wasn't careful, I'd start bawling all over again.

"So tell me," she said, clapping her hands and changing the subject, "how's the congressman?"

The congressman. Also known as my dad.

I shrugged. "As self-absorbed as ever. Bitter about the humiliation of his daughter bailing on her wedding. And pissed about all the money it cost him."

Marni scrunched up her face. "Would he rather you marry the wrong person?"

Did she really even need to ask that?

"Yes. Yes, he would. Plus, he seemed to like Vaughn. Maybe he'll adopt him and disown me."

She shook her head. "Families. Always a shit show."

She should know.

"The press was hounding me. It was awful," I said.

"What? Why did the press give a shit about your wedding? Or non-wedding?"

I shrugged one shoulder "Some election year bullshit. I don't completely understand it. You know I'm not into that political stuff. But the press can't find me here. At least I don't think so."

"All right. This is what we're gonna do tomorrow. We'll drop your car off at my mechanic, I'll take you by my gym, we'll have a nice workout, and we'll go for a drink afterward. Sound good?" she asked.

God. What an angel.

I stood as she clicked off the living room lights and we headed to our rooms.

"Sounds amazing. Love you, girl."

"Love you more."

3

____

Maze Abbott

Fuck if I wasn't in the world's shittiest mood.

Sure, I was part owner of Tableau, the hottest nightclub in Denver. But that gig came with more headaches than I ever could have imagined.

Take tonight, for example. It was Sunday. In the nightclub business, Sundays are slow. Not a lot of partying happened on Sunday nights. People had to get ready for the work week and all that.

But tonight? The club was freaking mobbed. And to make matters worse, both my business partners were off, my barback was missing in action, and one of our cocktail waitresses decided to get cramps.

I thought there was medication for that.

So I was busting my ass and probably wouldn't walk away with my usual purse of hefty tips because for some reason, people on Sunday were cheap fucks because they'd already blown through their weekend spending money.

So yeah, I might be inclined to throw a couple bottles or two against the wall. Not that I would. But I really wanted to.

"Hey, Maze," my friend Marni said, sliding onto a barstool just vacated by a sweet young thing with giant fake tits and a walking wallet sugar daddy.

"Hey," I said, eyeing the friend she'd brought along.

I'd never seen her before.

Yeah, a pretty girl could cheer me up as long as she wasn't one of those types who thought her looks would buy her a night of free drinks.

If I had a dollar for every woman who came in with that attitude, I'd be a rich man. Or rather, a poor man.

"Maze, this is my friend Stell. She just arrived from Philly," she said, gesturing to the woman who grabbed the stool next to her.

Stell smiled and extended her hand. "Nice to meet you."

Damn. Good, strong handshake. But warm, too.

"Hey. Welcome to Denver. You here for long?" I asked.

She looked at Marni and shrugged. "Not sure yet. I was going to just be stopping in on my way to LA, but... I had a fender bender and my car's in the shop now."

I pulled the tap to fill five glasses for a group of guys raising hell in a far corner. If they thought I was bringing these beers over to them, they could kiss my ass.

"Sorry to hear that, Stell. What can I get you ladies to drink?" I asked.

The two girls looked at each other.

I knew that look. They were sizing each other up to see how hard-core they wanted to go.

People did that, egg each other on.

I could hear the conversation in their heads.

Should we just have a glass of white wine?

Or should we go balls out with tequila shots?

It didn't matter to me, as long as they didn't drive.

"Do you drink martinis, Stell?" Marni asked.

There it was. She was laying out the challenge. Even if her friend had never had a martini in her life, she was going to have one now.

"Oh my god. *Martinis.* My dad drinks those," she said, rolling her eyes. "Let's do it."

They high fived each other, committing to a night of serious partying. They'd feel like shit tomorrow, that much I knew.

"Two vodka martinis up, with a twist," Marni declared, giggling.

Those were some of the easiest drinks I made. The ones with 'muddled' herbs and shit took forever, and drove me up a wall. That's why the fuckers were twenty dollars and up.

Yeah, twenty dollars for a goddamn drink. I wouldn't pay it, but plenty of people did.

In fact, I barely drank at all anymore. Neither did my business partners. When you're around booze all the time, it loses its appeal real fast—at least it did for me. Sometimes at the end of a long night, the very smell of alcohol could make me want to puke.

"Yo! Bartender," the jerks waiting for their beers hollered.

I knew they expected me to wait on their asses.

Wrong.

"Yo," I hollered back. "Your beers are right here. Getting warm, I might add."

That earned me some scowls. But I didn't care. I had their credit card.

Two of them got to their feet and sauntered over.

"Sorry guys," I said, lying out of my ass. I wasn't sorry. "We're short-staffed tonight."

"It's all good, bro," one of them said, balancing three glasses in his hands.

"Maze," Marni called. "We're ready for another round."

Damn. This could get ugly.

I leaned toward them. "Look, ladies. I usually mind my own business. But since I know you, Marni, and see you almost every day at the gym, I know you're some-what health conscious. So, before I pour you two another round, are you sure that's what you want? These martinis are awfully high-octane."

She looked at her friend as they silently egged each other on.

They both nodded enthusiastically.

As I figured they would.

"Thanks, Maze," she said. "Working alone tonight?"

I wiped down the bar with the disgusting towel I'd been using all night. Without a barback, it was almost impossible to keep the place neat and tidy. "Yeah. A couple people didn't show."

She held her glass up to me "Well, cheers. You're doing a kick ass job."

They giggled.

"So, Maze," Marni's friend said, "how long… have you had this… place?"

Christ, she wasn't even halfway through her second and she was already slurring.

"Coming up on three years."

For three years I'd been working my damn ass off. But I had to say, the money was fucking great. A few more years of this, and I could take my tired ass down to the Caribbean if I wanted to.

Although my business partners would probably lose their shit if I bailed.

I got to work polishing the glasses just coming out of the dishwasher, my absolute least favorite job in the world. But without a barback, the water spots weren't going to come out on their own.

What was further fucking with my mood was that I was dreading tomorrow. The club was closed on Mondays, which meant inventory and other paperwork had to be tackled. My partners and I rotated these tasks, and it was my turn. That shit was deadly boring, and I was about the least detail-oriented person in the world. I always managed to screw something up. I was surprised they still even let me do the shit, that's how many times I'd messed up.

I wasn't doing it on purpose, with the hope they'd give up on me and do it themselves.

Honest.

The one saving grace about Monday, though, was that I got to teach my bartending class. Now, that got me out of bed in the morning. It was lively and fun, and we always had a great time. So, all was not lost.

"Um, Maze?" Marni's friend called.

Their glasses were empty.

"That is your name, right? Maze," she asked, dragging it out slowly.

Well. I hadn't looked at her long enough to notice her gorgeous eyes, a sort of light brown with a dark ring around the edges of the iris. They angled up on the outer edges, giving her a slightly exotic appearance.

"Maze?" she asked again.

"Oh. Yeah, sorry."

Busted for staring.

"Yes, Maze is my name. What's yours again? Stella?"

She shook her head. "Just *Stell*."

Jesus. I was going to have to get the scoop on this one from Marni later.

She held up her glass, clumsily waving it around. "We're ready for another round," she sang.

They leaned into each other and giggled again.

"All right, ladies."

I knew better than to offer any advice. Once people had started drinking and the buzz set in, the 'maybe I should stop now' sensibility sailed right out the window.

Three martinis each? They were going to be a fucking mess.

And they were.

4

____

Maze

IT WAS COMING up on nine o'clock, which was when we closed on Sunday. Most of our patrons had left, except a few stragglers like Marni and Stell.

"Maze," Marni slurred. "Can we get one more each? Please?" she begged, pushing her empty glass toward me.

"I'm going to the bathroom," Stell said in a garbled voice. "Which way?"

Marni pointed. "Up the stairs."

We watched her stumble across the floor, reaching for every table and chair along the way that might possibly help her balance.

Marni shook her head happily. "Love that girl. She's

my *ride or die bitch*. Seriously. Always has been. Always will be. You know what I mean, Maze?" she asked, tearing up.

Christ. The last thing I wanted to deal with was a crying drunk.

"Hey, Marni, I was thinking, maybe you've had enough—"

"Nonsense!" she yelled.

Okay, she was going from teary-eyed to belligerent. Great.

I turned back to putting liquor bottles in a locked cage, hoping to stall for Stell's return. Surely I could talk some sense into her.

Right?

"Oh shit, Marni," she said when she'd made her way back to the bar. "I used the men's room. It was closer."

"That's what I fucking love about you, Stell. You just make shit happen."

I didn't see how using the men's room was *making shit happen*, but I wasn't going to ask.

"No, no, no, Marn," Stell babbled. "I fucking love you, *girl*."

Oh yeah. They were definitely being cut off.

"Okay, you two. I'm cashing you out and calling you an Uber."

They looked at me like I'd said their baby was ugly.

"Oh, Maze," Marni said, leaning on the bar with her hand extended toward me. "Don't be that way."

"Sorry, ladies. It's time to go."

They looked at each other with such utter indignation it was comical.

And I was not in a laughing mood.

"C'mon, Maze. I just got to town. My car was smashed. I need a fucking break here."

They weren't going down easy.

I leaned onto the bar, looking from one to the other. "The answer is no."

Stell slammed her hand on the bar. "Well, shit. Marn, you told me this place was cool. Let's get outta here." She stumbled as she got to her feet, and Marni grabbed her arm.

"If you wait a few minutes, I can drive you ladies home."

"I'll wait if you get me another martini," Stell said in a singsong voice.

"Sorry, ladies."

I gestured to the lone busboy tasked with cleaning the place up after hours. "Can you lock up for me? I'm taking off."

He saluted me. "Sure, boss. Gotcha covered."

Stell's head bobbled. "Well, fuck you then," she slurred.

"Yeah, Maze. Go to hell," Marni mumbled.

Really?

"C'mon, ladies, I'm taking you home."

In spite of their blustering, they obediently followed me to my car. I opened the back door, and stuffed both of them in.

"Seatbelts, please," I said, watching them clumsily help each other.

It would be funny if I weren't in such a shit mood.

When we reached Marni's place, Stell leaned over the seat to see me. "Hey. Maze. You wanna come in?"

Oh, for Christ's sake.

"Nah. I'm good. You ladies have a nice rest of the night."

Stell's mouth dropped open. "Oh. Well. Fine." She got out of the car and slammed the door so hard she lost her balance and wiped out on the grass in front of Marni's building.

Marni bent to help her friend up, and the two of them went down.

But they were home, and I'd done my part. I drove away, my last glance in the rear-view mirror showing they'd tentatively gotten to their feet.

Fucking shit show.

ON MY WAY back to Tableau the next day, I did a drive by at the gym for a quick cardio workout.

And no one was more surprised than I was to see Marni there, working.

"Maze," she mumbled. "Morning." She took my ID card and swiped it.

"You look like shit, Marni," I said, hiking my back-pack up on my shoulder.

She leaned on the front desk and brought a water bottle to her lips. After chugging half of it, she wiped her mouth with the back of her hand. "Thanks, Maze. That's very kind."

One of her employees approached her about a clog in the women's locker room bathroom, and she just squinted at them.

But she was the boss, so it was her problem. Just like she'd been my problem the night before. She probably didn't even recall half of it.

"Hey, Maze," she called, beckoning me with her finger. She lowered her voice. "Did we... misbehave last night?"

I nodded. "Sure did."

I left her wondering exactly what she'd done, and headed for the men's locker room. I wasn't in the mood for the kind of apology you got from a customer the day after overdoing it.

But on my way, I spotted Stell wandering through the weight room, like she wasn't sure where to start.

And fuck, was she cute in some gray leggings and a white cut-off T-shirt that showed off her flat belly.

I stood out of sight to see what she would do.

First, she sat on one of the huge exercise balls. Then, she wrinkled her nose and lay down on a mat. But after deciding that wouldn't do, she got up and took a hula hoop off the wall and actually started twirling it around her waist.

As she did, the ponytail on top of her head swung

around and her curvy ass jiggled the tiniest amount under the thin layer of spandex covering it. She rocked back and forth like a champ, showing no signs of a hangover, unlike her friend Marni.

I hadn't expected that.

She raised her arms above her head and got lost in the motion. I was stunned. That hula hoop had hung on the gym wall for as long as I'd been a member, and I'd never seen anyone use it.

She was so unselfconscious, enjoying herself, that I couldn't look away.

Until she caught me.

She stopped short, and the hoop clattered to the floor.

That was my sign to get a move on.

She might be cute, but she was a mess. And I didn't do messes.

5

Stell

"Is this Miss Estella Kline?"

I bolted up in bed. The person on the other end of the line sounded Official. Very Official.

I smoothed the comforter over my lap and pushed my hair out of my face as if someone could see me.

"This is she," I said.

"Miss Kline, this is Dan calling from Statehouse Insurance."

Hmmm. Never heard of them.

"Yes?"

"Well, it looks like you got into an automobile accident with a Mr. Robbins Stryker a few days ago?"

Oh, that's what this was about. I hoped it wouldn't

take them long to cut my check. I had a long way to travel to get to LA and time was wasting.

I loved staying at Marni's. I really did. Her amazing condo was positively dreamy with its chef's kitchen, sprawling living room with fireplace, and balcony off every bedroom.

It was better than the Four Seasons. Not that I'd ever stayed at the Four Seasons.

But a new life awaited me in LA, one far away from Vaughn and the wedding I'd called off, far away from my pissed and humiliated parents, and far away from my job as a kindergarten teacher that I'd never been much good at, anyway.

"Yes, Mr. Stryker did *strike* my car." I giggled.

The pun went over Dan's head.

"Miss Kline, there is a discrepancy between your story and Mr. Stryker's about the specifics of the accident, and therefore which party is responsible. Until this is resolved, there will be no insurance payout."

Oh no. That wouldn't work for me. Not at all.

"Dan, I'm not sure you are aware, but I'm on my way to LA. Los Angeles. You see, I had some rough times at home in Philly—Philadelphia—and needed to head west for a change. I got as far as Denver, as you know, but I need to continue on my journey. There are big things waiting for me in LA, Dan."

I could be persuasive when I had to.

He probably needed my bank account info to forward me the money for the repair. I grabbed my purse off my nightstand and pulled out my checkbook to read him the routing and account numbers.

"That sounds wonderful Miss Kline, but until fault is established, no payments will be made."

He hadn't understood me at all.

"Dan, maybe I wasn't clear, but I need my car to be repaired so I can continue to LA. And in order to get my car repaired, I need the money to pay the people fixing it. In fact, Dan, it's in the shop right now, being fixed. You know what I mean?"

Papers shuffled in the background, and if I wasn't mistaken, Dan sighed deeply. "I'm sorry. We have to work through the process of assigning fault. Now if you don't have any other questions—"

I tried to control my voice, but it crept an octave or two higher anyway. "Dan, I need that money. I need the money to fix my car. Rob… Stryker, or whatever his name is, hit my car. He smashed the shit out of it, if you want to know the truth, and I don't have the money to get it fixed. That's why I need your insurance company to pay for the damage he inflicted."

Was it too late to claim neck pain? Shit, why hadn't I thought of that when Mister State Trooper was on hand?

"I'm sorry. We aren't paying for anything until this is resolved."

No, no, no.

"Dan. Where am I supposed to GET THE FUCKING MONEY TO PAY FOR MY CAR?"

Silence.

"We'll be back in touch when we know more."

And the line went dead.

Was he *kidding*?

Some asshole hits my car, and it's not absolutely clear that he was the one who fucked up?

I jumped out of bed and pulled on the plushy pink robe Marni had loaned me.

"Marn," I hollered.

Coffee bubbled in the kitchen.

"Oh my god, Marn," I said, rushing toward her.

She stopped mid-pour. "Coffee?"

I nodded. "Marn, you won't believe what I have to tell you—"

She raised her arms and shushed me. "Wait. Wait. Now come here. Look at what a beautiful day it is," she exclaimed, opening the shutters on the span of glass providing a view of Denver and the mountains beyond.

"I don't care how beautiful it is outside," I snapped.

She wrinkled her nose. "Is something wrong, Stell?"

Oh my god. I loved her but I was about to kill her.

So I spoke as fast as I could, before she interrupted me again. "The insurance company is not paying me. At least not yet."

Her eyes widened. "Oh, no."

The frustration of the non-conversation with Dan suddenly bubbled up in my chest, and my bottom lip quivered.

"I don't have the money to pay for the repair myself,

and if insurance doesn't pay, I can't get to LA." I plopped down on one of her kitchen counter stools and buried my head in my hands.

"Fuck, fuck, fuck. I should have known something like this would happen. It's karma. I have fucked up karma for all the horrible things I've done in my life."

Marni rubbed a hand over my back. "You haven't done anything horrible, honey, except maybe leave Vaughn at the altar."

I nodded, the tears flowing. "That was big one. But not the only one."

"Well, what else have you done?" she asked gently.

"I don't know," I sniffed. "I shoplifted some gum, once."

I heard a snicker that was promptly extinguished. "Um, Stell, how old were you when you did that?"

"Ten. Maybe twelve."

"Stell, are you saying you're broke?"

I hated for her to know what a loser I was. But if she didn't know by now, since we'd been friends most of our lives, she needed to.

I nodded. "Yeah."

"Come with me while I dress for work."

I followed her to her bedroom, my head hanging in shame and watched her pull a uniform of black workout pants and a fitted, racerback tank on her perfect figure. She topped it off with a cropped black hoodie with the name of the gym on it—Altitude

Fitness. So appropriate for the mile-high city of Denver.

"We need a plan, Stell. I can make some calls for you, but for the short term, I can find something for you to do at the gym, where you can make a little money. It won't be much, but it's a start."

No. Way.

"You can get me a job at Altitude? Are you kidding?"

Altitude was the most exclusive gym in the entire Denver metroplex. At least that's what Marni had told me.

She laughed. "Of course I can hire you. I own the joint. Now go get dressed and we'll be on our way."

"Oh my god, Marn, I love you," I screamed, almost knocking her over with a hug.

"Okay, okay," she said, peeling my arms from around her neck. "We need to hurry. I don't like being late, it sets a bad example for the rest of the team."

I rushed to my room and pulled on the same gym clothes I'd worn the day before, without even stopping to see if they stank. I didn't have time to worry about details. I was a big picture person now, and I was visualizing LA with its palm trees, beaches, and movie stars.

In fact, while Marni drove us to Altitude, I scrolled through my Pinterest pin board of LA pictures. I tried to look at them every day to manifest my dream.

So far, I was halfway there. That was the positive way to look at things.

When we arrived, I was so excited, I was bouncing in my sneakers. "Okay. Tell me what you need me to do. I'll do anything you need, Marn."

She looked at me with a raised eyebrow. "We need all the dirty towels emptied out of the bins in the workout rooms, and brought to the laundry in the basement."

What?

Dirty towels? Basement?

"Oh. Okay," I said.

She pulled a wheeled cart out of a closet. "Don't forget to get the ones in the women's locker room. We'll get one of the guys to get the ones from the men's locker room later."

I pushed the cart towards the first towel bin I saw.

"Wait," she called after me. "Here, put on this shirt so you look like an employee. And wear these gloves. You never know what people might have."

Oh god.

I pushed the cart as my hands sweated in the cheap disposable gloves, retrieving towels that looked like they'd never been used, and some that looked like whoever had used them hadn't bathed in weeks.

More than once I held my breath.

Wow. Was this what the universe had intended for me? It could be. I'd read that sometimes you got knocked down before your big win came. It was called *paying your dues.*

And I was paying the shit out of my dues.

I'd brought my first load of towels to the basement, when I ran into Marni. I tried to smile bravely.

"How's it going? This is so cool. We're working together," she exclaimed.

Yeah. So cool.

"Hey, Marn, see that guy over there with the free weights?"

She craned her neck. "With the tattoos?"

"Yes, exactly. Is it possible that's Adam Levine?" I asked quietly.

She nudged me. "Oh yeah. That's totally him. We get celebs in here all the time. See, I didn't create the top gym in Denver for the movers and shakers to go somewhere else." Smacking me on the back, she laughed and walked away.

The place had quite the crowd. She wasn't kidding. I'd never seen such a collection of flawless men and women, none of whom seemed to be breaking much of a sweat as they kept their toned bodies in top shape.

I lowered my head when I passed Adam Levine. Even though he had no idea who I was, I didn't want him to know I was going through a loser patch in my life. I was sure he'd been there at one point or another, like when Maroon 5 was trying to get off the ground, and that he could probably relate to my challenges. But now was not the time to get into it. He looked busy.

Plus, I was supposed to be working.

As I filled a second cart with dirty towels, I passed an announcements board that listed all the gym's classes—spin, yoga, weightlifting, basketball—when I spotted a little flyer about yoga teacher training.

Holy shit. Just what I needed.

What I didn't need, on the other hand, was the eight hundred dollar price tag.

And as if seeing Adam Levine at my lowest moment wasn't bad enough, who did I spot on the treadmill but Maze, the bartender from Tableau, who'd cut Marni and me off for getting a little tipsy.

I ducked behind a pillar so I could watch him.

Cripes, I'd known he was hot the night he served us at his club, but now that he was full-on running, drenched in sweat in a T-shirt clinging to his muscles and occasionally dabbing his forehead with the white gym towel around his shoulders, I could see how freaking gorgeous he was.

He pressed a couple buttons on his machine, and it began to slow. He did that thing people on treadmills do, where they jump on the sides of it while it winds down, and stepped off the machine.

Shit. I didn't want him to see me. I mean, Adam Levine had probably seen me, but he didn't know me.

And now he was headed straight for me.

Oh my god oh my god.

The pillar I was hiding behind would serve me for only a few more seconds.

"Hey, Maze, how's it going?" a female voice called.

I peeked to find he'd turned to greet a tall, impossibly thin woman with long, blonde hair.

"Oh. Hi, Annabel."

While his back was to me, I took the opportunity to exit with my nearly full cart. I practically ran to the elevator that would take me to the basement, hiding my face until the doors closed, protecting me from the humiliation of the 'perfects' of the world, accepting that I was anything but.

Stell

I DIDN'T HAVE the heart to tell Marni that even though she'd hooked me up with a job when I was about as down and out as I'd ever been, I thought I should keep my eyes open for an opportunity better than collecting dirty towels at her club.

And I'd found something particularly interesting on Craigslist that morning. I responded to an ad for a hostess, and immediately got a call.

Wow. Guess they really needed someone fast.

"Hello," I said in my most hostess-like voice.

"Is this Estella?" a deep voice asked.

I slipped my bedroom door closed. I didn't want Marni to hear me.

"Yes," I said breezily. "But you can call me Stell."

"Great. Can you come in for an interview today?" the man asked.

"Of course. Could we do it later in the day, though? I have one other interview earlier," I lied.

It was good to seem in demand.

"Sure. What time you wanna come by?"

I paused as if I were checking my calendar. "How is three p.m.?"

"Super. I'll text you the address. See you then."

"Oh, before you go, can I get your name—"

But he was gone. Geez.

"Hey, Marn," I said as we were on the way to the gym.

She'd told me they were going to pay me 'under the table.' I got the impression a lot of people in the gym were paid that way.

"Couple things," I started. "First, I will need to leave a little early today… to talk to the mechanic about my car."

Ugh. I didn't like lying to her.

"Sure. No problem" she said, glancing over at me with a smile.

She pulled into the parking garage under Altitude.

"And I thought I could give you some ideas I have for the gym. You know, to streamline operations and such."

She pressed her lips together and side-eyed me.

"Now, wait until you've heard my ideas, Marn. Be open-minded."

She avoided my gaze while we rode up in the elevator.

I continued. "I was thinking that instead of having someone make the rounds all day long picking up towels, that you could install a chute, where the members could drop them, and they'd go right to the laundry room."

I waited for her to tell me the idea was brilliant.

But she didn't.

She pulled me aside after we'd exited the elevator. "Stell. I'm glad you're thinking about these things. I really am. But I'm not sure this arrangement is going to work out. You know, my dad always said not to hire friends, at least those who you value. And you know how much I value you."

"What? Are you firing me?" I asked, my voice cracking.

She looked across the room and waved at someone. "I wouldn't really say that. Now, if you'll excuse me, I need to check in with the front desk manager. Have a great day, sweetie."

Shit.

"Hi. We spoke earlier today. I'm here for the hostess interview."

A burly guy with black hairs sprouting from his nostrils gestured for me to take the seat opposite his desk.

Once I had, and could see him a bit more clearly, I found he also had black hairs growing out of the sides of his ears.

Don't stare. Don't stare.

But I couldn't take my eyes off his nose hairs. Didn't he know he could easily trim those?

"So, Estella—"

I raised my hand. "Stell. Call me Stell."

He took a deep breath. "Stell, how long have you been in Denver?"

"I just arrived a few days ago." I'd decided not to tell any prospective employers I was on my way to LA. I didn't want to hurt my chances.

His face brightened. "That's great. Welcome to Denver."

Geez. Everyone here was so nice. Not at all like the East Coast.

"So we have a private club, Stell. And we need escorts for the club. Our clients are high rollers, people who fly in from all over the world."

I leaned forward in my seat. "I thought the job was for a hostess."

He waved his hand. "Oh yeah. Well, that's what we have to call it in Craigslist. We can't come right out and say we're looking for escorts."

Well, that made sense. I guess.

"So what kind of escorts do your clients need? Someone to show them around the city and such? Because you know I've just arrived, and I don't know my way around *at all*."

Confusion washed across his face. "No, they don't need to be shown around. They want *escorts*."

He said it with emphasis, as if that might help me understand better.

But I didn't.

"It pays very well. You get sixty percent of the fee, and the house gets forty."

Huh?

Oh.

Wait.

Was he talking about what I thought he was?

No. No way.

"Um. Do you mean, like, I would, um… like have sex with these men?"

There. I'd said it. Best to be straightforward. That's the only way to manifest what you want.

He rolled his eyes. "What the hell else do you think an escort does?"

Right. That's exactly what they do. It *was* a dumb question.

I popped to my feet and started backing toward the door. "I think I misunderstood what you needed. I'm gonna head out now."

I pulled the door open.

"Hey, before you go, do you know of anybody else who might be interested—"

But I didn't hear the rest of the question. I dashed home in an Uber and as soon as I got arrived at Marni's, opened a pint of maple walnut ice cream, and got in bed.

7

Robbins "Robbie" Stryker

"Hey Marni. Heard you had quite the good time sitting here at the bar the other night."

She put a hand over her eyes and shook her head. "It was not my finest hour. If Maze doesn't absolutely hate me, I will consider that a win."

I continued setting up my garnishes. It was going to be a busy night and I didn't want to stop in the middle of it to cut up fucking lemons and limes. "Well, you're lucky we like you. And that you own the gym we go to. We'd never jeopardize our memberships." I'd said that as a joke, but there was a lot of truth to it.

A membership at Altitude was worth its weight in gold.

She took a seat on a barstool, laughing. "Thank god I can hang Altitude over your head. At least I have something going for myself. Well that, and the fact that my brother works here."

I wiped the bar in front of her and laid out a coaster. "Can I get you anything?"

She shook her head, her hair swinging around her face. She had an interesting look for someone who ran a gym. She was more rock 'n roll than jock. But that was one of the things I admired about her. And because she was sister to one of my business partners, she was like a sister to me. I'd briefly considered trying to get romantic with her, but I knew her brother wouldn't be able to deal.

Just as well.

She put her hands up. I had a feeling she'd be off alcohol for a while. "No thanks. I'm just stopping by. I'll take some water, though."

"Coming right up."

She looked around the club. "I love this place when it's quiet. Reminds me of a monster that's yet to come alive."

I had to laugh at that one. I'd not heard Tableau described that way, but it wasn't far off the mark.

"Hey, speaking of the gym, why haven't I seen you there in a while?" she asked.

I sighed. My life had been a shit show of epic proportion of late. "Jax's baby momma is not making my life easy. In fact, she's hell-bent on making it as shitty as she can. Never mind how it might affect the baby."

My son Jax. The most amazing thing to ever happen to me. Knocking up his psycho mother on our second date? Not so much.

"How is the little guy?" she asked.

It was incredible how turning my thoughts to him made any other issue in my life melt away.

"He's wonderful. Trying to crawl. Half the time looks like a turtle stuck on his stomach."

Marni laughed. "I need to see him soon. We'll put together some sort of get-together when everyone is free."

Which meant we'd never have a get-together. With our schedules at Tableau, and Marni's at Altitude, the chances of our times off coinciding were almost zero. But that was okay. Our paths continued to cross all the time.

"So, Robbie, I came by to talk to you about something," she said.

I stopped cleaning and gave her my attention. "What's up?"

"I have a friend who's in town on a short-term basis and she needs some work. Do you guys have anything for her?"

Hmmm. The timing on this might be just right. Maze had been bitching about people not showing up for their shifts. We had to cut the no-shows loose.

Cold? Yeah. But we were trying to run a business

and one or two people flaking threw everything else out of whack.

"Is she reliable?" I asked.

Marni shook her head enthusiastically.

She'd better not be bullshitting me. I know what it was like to want to help a friend. You'll do anything for them. Including telling white lies.

"We need a new barback."

She frowned momentarily, then went back to smiling. "Oh. That would be great. She'd love it."

Yeah. Not so fast.

"Is she strong? She'd have to lift twenty pounds or so several times a night."

She nodded again. "Oh yes. She's very strong. Works out all the time."

Okay. Marni had no idea what a barback was. No one would ever sign their friend up for such a shit job, basically being a busboy to whomever was tending bar. There was a reason we went through them so fast, and that they so often didn't show. There was nothing about it that was fun.

They were more or less bar gophers and they had to moving fucking fast when we were busy.

I shrugged. "Okay. Tell her to come in tomorrow at five. I'll train her and we'll see how she does."

Marni popped off her barstool and jumped up and down, clapping her hands.

Jesus, this friend must really need the work.

"Thank you so much Robbie! You won't regret this."

She glanced at her watch. "Gotta get back to Altitude. I have some new yoga teachers coming in."

Damn. I had a thing for yoga teachers. They were always so fit, and wore the skimpiest clothes. And then there were all the ways they could bend…

"See ya," she called, running for the door.

"WELL IF IT isn't Denver's Most Eligible Bachelor," I called to Maze, knowing it would bug the shit out of him.

He scowled like I knew he would. "Keep it down, Rob. The last thing I need is for everyone to find out about that stupid shit."

Laughing, I clapped him on the back. "Dude, everyone already knows. What's the problem? Think of all the pussy you're gonna get. And it's great for the club."

"Well. There is that."

He started making a nasty looking muddled cocktail that a girl at the end of the bar had ordered. And that wasn't all she wanted.

She was practically drooling watching him make it.

"I hate making these drinks," he muttered.

Seriously. You'd think charging twenty-plus dollars for them would put people off. But when something was 'in,' people would pay whatever it took.

"So who is the private party for tonight?" I asked.

He shook his head. "It's being hosted by that Grant guy. But I don't like it. He's bad news. Fights always break out when he and his posse are here. I'm just waiting to hear gunfire someday. I wouldn't put it past him."

He walked to the end of the bar to deliver the muddled cocktail, and while he was getting the woman's credit card, she ran her hand up his arm, muttering something about his tattoos.

Maze was not a fan of that shit. He could be pretty cranky. Actually, he was cranky most every day of his life.

"Why does Deb keep letting them book the Playroom if they're nothing but trouble?" I asked.

He shook his head. "I think she's afraid to say no."

"Hey, don't look now, but Annabel is working tonight," I said, gesturing discreetly.

Maze slammed the cash drawer, catching his finger, and responding with a loud *fuck*. "Yeah. I know. I saw the schedule."

Keeping her eyes on Maze from across the room, Annabel tied on her waiter's apron and twisted her hair into a high ponytail. I had to hand it to her. She might be a psycho, but she was beautiful.

And she sure did have a thing for Maze.

It bordered on obsession. And I don't know if she was aware or not, but she was inches away from getting fired. She'd harassed him too many times.

"She still bothering you, man?" I asked.

He avoided looking in her direction. "Yeah. When I came out of the gym the other day, there was another note on my car."

Shit.

Maze wiped his hands on a bar towel and looked around. "You know what? It's not too busy yet. Let me go up to the office to continue working on the schedule. Buzz me if you need anything."

"Sure thing, man. Hey, one thing before you go."

He turned to face me. "What's up?"

"I may have to leave early tomorrow to get Jax. His mother is doing everything she can to make my life as difficult as possible."

"No problem. How's all that going?"

My mood brightened again. The little bugger had that effect on me. "The baby is awesome. His mother is not."

That about summed it up.

Jax's mother Elise had arranged for *her* mother to babysit most days when she and I had to work. But every now and then, Elise's mom was unavailable, and I would take him since I had the more flexible schedule. But it always happened at the last minute, and on the club's busiest days of the week.

A coincidence?

Doubt it.

"Well good luck with that drama," Maze said.

Yeah, thanks.

8

Robbie

Contrary to expectations, the night had *not* been busy, and as a result, it just crept by. I preferred being swamped. It made the time go by faster. And it was more lucrative.

And because it had been on the slow side, Maze spent the entire night up in the office, doing paperwork. I couldn't blame him. He needed to steer clear of Annabel.

And, less than twelve hours later, I was back at the helm, having come in early so I could leave early to get my kid.

"Excuse me. I'm here about a job. As a barback."

Awesome. I turned around to welcome the person I figured was Marni's friend—

Holy shit.

Was this a joke?

"Oh my god," she said.

Oh my god was right. Shit, shit, shit.

Narrowing her eyes, she pointed a finger at me. "*You're* the guy who smashed my car the other day. And if that's not bad enough, now you're denying it was your fault."

"Are… are you Marni's friend?"

No way. There was just no way Marni's friend was the woman whose car I'd rear-ended.

"I sure am. And I'm the person whose car you fucked up. Thanks to you, my trip to LA has been put on hold, and I now have to work in Denver for god knows how long so I can pay for its repair." Her voice was growing progressively louder. "Because *you* won't take responsibility for what you did."

She slammed her hand on the bar, apparently not done. "I can't believe you're a friend of Marni's. How is such a nice person friends with a crook like you?"

I held my hands up. "Hey, hey, hey. You need to settle down."

"What?" she spat. "Settle down? Why? Because you're mister cool club guy and can fuck over anyone you want?"

That's not really how it was, but I had a feeling it wasn't the best time to try and explain that.

"Okay, look. What's your name?" I asked.

She was way more beautiful than I'd realized that dark night.

"Don't you know my name? It was all over the driver's license I had to share with you, *Robbins*."

"I don't go by Robbins. I go by Robbie. And you must be Estella."

"Stell. The name is Stell. Tell me, where do you get off fucking someone over like this—"

I held my hands up. "Wait. Listen to me for one minute. The club is about to get busy. Do you want to work, or do you want to lecture me all night?"

I hoped she'd stick around, no matter how disagreeable she was. I needed the help.

She pressed her lips together and scanned the room. The club was starting to fill up, and I needed her to either get to work, or hit the road.

"Stell, can we call a truce and get to work? I promise we can hammer this out later tonight."

Her bottom lip quivered.

And I felt like a dick.

"Fine. We can just stay out of each other's way," she snapped.

Sounded like Marni hadn't told Stell what a barback was. Either that, or she didn't know. Because Stell didn't, either.

"Well now, that won't exactly work. You and I will be working pretty closely together tonight."

She rolled her eyes. "Great. Just great. But let's get

this show on the road. I'm ready to start. So I can pay for the car you so cavalierly wrecked."

Was I going to hear of nothing else the entire night?

"Okay. Let's get started. First, come back here behind the bar. I'll show you what you need to do."

She scrunched her face. "Behind the bar? I thought I was waiting tables."

Uh oh.

"I guess Marni didn't tell you we needed a barback. Not a waitress."

She nodded. "Yeah. That's what she told me."

"So… I guess you don't know what a barback is," I said, grimacing.

She threw her hands up in the air. She was a feisty one.

Her eyebrows rose and she put her hands on her hips. "Are you going to tell me? Or should we pass the night playing guessing games?"

She hustled down to the end of the bar and I lifted the hinged counter to let her in. And holy shit, if she wasn't wearing some nice duds.

Rule number one of barbacks. Do not wear nice clothing.

I handed her an apron. "You'd better cover up that pretty blouse. You're going to get dirty tonight."

Now that she was standing right in front of me, I had to admit I couldn't look away from her bewitching brown eyes. And I was usually a blue eye kind of guy.

"Go ahead. Put it on."

She took it gingerly from me, as if it were contaminated.

"All right. A barback is basically a busboy, just for the bartender. You will be fetching buckets of ice, replenishing the coolers of beer when we run low, running glassware through the dishwasher, and just generally making sure the bar is clean. Here's a towel for you. I normally tuck them into my—"

She shook her head in disbelief. "Are you serious? *That's* what I'm going to be doing tonight?"

I was running out of time—and patience—to keep arguing. "Do you want this job or not? Because if you can't handle it, you need to leave now."

She snapped her mouth shut.

I took a deep breath. "Okay. I need you to start cutting fruit. We need about a dozen lemons, limes, and oranges. They're right over here," I said, leading her to a clear spot next to the cash register where a giant bin of fruit waited.

I hesitated before giving her a knife, that's how fucking bent out of shape she was. But I did, against my better judgment.

She snatched it out of my hand, glared at me, and walked over to the fruit.

She probably wouldn't be back tomorrow, if she even finished out the night. Nobody liked being a barback, unless they really needed the money.

Or their car had just been smashed by an asshole like me.

9

Stell

OH MY FUCKING GOD. Had I done *that* much wrong in my life to deserve the plateful of bullshit I'd been served starting the very moment I'd driven into Denver, Colorado?

Did every new person in this town wander around with a black cloud hanging over their head? Or was I the only one?

And when was it going to freaking end?

I'd been in a car wreck.

I'd been offered a job as a prostitute.

I'd been fired by my best friend.

And now I was a bar bitch.

Where, incidentally, I worked with the very asshole

who'd wrecked my car. And who was trying to weasel out of paying for the damage he'd caused.

I *knew* it. I should have stayed in Philly. Even married Vaughn, despite the fact that he was a self-centered, cheating-ass douchebag.

All my visualizations of Los Angeles, with its swaying palm trees, white sand beaches, celebrity sightings, and endless fresh sushi had done nothing except get me stranded halfway across the country.

Granted, I was with my best friend. There was that.

But I was never going to get to LA. I'd have to go back home, stay at my parents' until I got some money saved, and return to teaching kindergarten.

"Hey," the Car Wrecker, said. "Do you know how to change a keg?"

I straightened up from where I'd crawled under the bar to pick up the box of straws I'd dropped all over the place.

Why'd he have to be so damn good-looking with his man bun, nerd glasses, and perfectly sculpted jawline? Why couldn't he be short, fat, bald, and have warts on his face?

The universe was so fucking unfair.

I put my hands on my hips.

I didn't say anything. I didn't need to.

Do I look like I fucking know how to change a keg?

Without a word, he got the message loud and clear.

"All right. Take the hand truck into the cooler, grab

a new keg of Sierra Nevada, and bring it here. I'll show you how to hook it up."

Goody.

I had no idea how I'd identify a keg of Sierra Nevada, nor put it on a hand truck. Such was my new job.

I limped, because I'd made the mistake of wearing my cute boots, through a set of double doors, where I found the cooler Robbie had shown me earlier. I entered the giant refrigerator, propping the door open with a chair so I didn't get trapped, and immediately found a keg with a big Sierra Nevada sticker on it.

Victory.

But not so fast.

Turns out kegs are heavy. Like really heavy. And I wasn't able to budge the one I wanted. So, being the problem solver that I am, I tipped the bad boy over on its side with a loud *bam!* and rolled it onto the hand truck. I backed both out of the cooler, where they banged down the cooler step-up and onto the floor, and I wheeled the whole mess back to the bar.

"Good job. Look at you," Robbie said as I maneuvered my awkward charge to the small refrigerator behind the bar where he'd pulled out what I assumed was an empty.

"Whew," I said, wiping my brow. "I think I shook it up a bit."

That was an understatement.

"No worries. It always happens. Okay, pay close

attention." He wedged the new keg into the fridge, something I was pretty sure I'd never be able to do, and then started attaching various hoses.

"Okay. Carbon dioxide flows into the keg *here*, and pushes the beer out of this valve *here* and up and into the tap."

Wow. I had no idea that's how they worked.

"This piece of equipment, that does both these things, is called a coupler."

"Where does the carbon dioxide come from?" I asked.

He raised his eyebrows. "Good question. There are tanks on the other side of this," he said, pointing to the wall holding shelves of liquor bottles.

"So complicated," I muttered.

"It's not so bad. Pretty soon you'll be able to do this on your own. In a minute we'll pour a glass to make sure the beer's not too foamy."

God. He was being nice. Maybe making up for trying to rip me off?

"Thanks," I said, looking at the crowd queuing to order drinks. "Guess you better get back to it. The wolves are at the door."

He looked around. "No kidding. Now, if you can bring about five containers of ice using this empty pickle bucket to fill up the ice machine over here, that would be great."

Was he fucking kidding? I was hauling ice now?

"Why do you add ice to an ice machine? Doesn't it just make ice for you?" I asked.

He smiled. "It does, but when we're busy, it can't keep up."

He thrust the white bucket at me and ran to wait on the thirsty hordes.

Well, shit. Were they going to ask me to scrub the toilets, too?

But I reminded myself to keep my eye on the ball. LA might be slipping further and further out of sight, but I had shorter-term goals like getting my car fixed and maybe enrolling in the yoga teacher training at Altitude. I was hoping Marni would give me a little break on the fee. It was the least she could do since she'd fired me and set me up with this sweet shitball of a job.

I survived the night. Somehow, someway, I did all the dirty work thrown at me and then some, and I could swear, Tableau never had a cleaner bar than when they'd set me loose on the place.

Someone set a beer down, leaving a wet ring? I was on top of that so fast the bar never knew what was coming. We were getting low on lime wedges? I had the bin refilled before anyone noticed. Running out of ice? Boom, done.

Finally, things began to slow. A tall, blonde waitress who'd ignored me all night stood at the end of the bar, and gestured me over.

Hey, I'd seen her at the gym, talking to Maze.

"Hi. I'm Stell," I said, extending my hand.

Would she be my first 'work friend'?

"Where's Maze?" she demanded.

Guess not.

"Oh. I don't know." Why was she asking *me*? "In the office, I guess."

She rolled her eyes, and next thing I knew, Robbie was beside me.

"Annabel. Do you need something?" he asked.

She pointed to the opposite end of the bar. "You have a customer," she said, smiling sweetly.

As soon as Robbie was gone, her smile faded. "Look. I'm going to tell you only once. Stay away from Maze. He's mine."

What the hell?

"Um, Annabel, I have no interest in Maze—"

She leaned closer. "You heard me." She straightened back up and with a flick of her wrist, 'accidentally' knocked over a beer, which poured all down the inside of the bar and over some clean glasses.

10

Stell

HOLY SHIT.

"You did that on purpose, you jerk—"

"What's going on here?" Robbie demanded, appearing from behind me.

"Oh my god. You should have seen what she just did—"

He waved Annabel away. "Go. Get out of here before you make any more trouble."

She smirked at me and slunk away.

She thought she could get away with that kind of bullshit? Don't think so.

Robbie grabbed a rag and started wiping up the beer. "Sorry about that. She's pretty much our resident psycho. Can you wipe off those glasses down there?" he asked.

I'd already started cleaning up Psycho's mess. "I'd say she's the resident *bitch*. But that's just me."

Robbie leaned closer, and I had to admit he smelled damn good. Pretty much just plain soap, mixed with the scent of a guy who'd been working hard. It was quite pleasant after smelling beer and booze all night. I took a deep breath.

He looked at me like I was a weirdo.

Oops.

"Look, don't tell her things like where Maze is. She's trouble and he keeps away from her. I called the office and told Maze to lock the door."

I nearly dropped the glass I was holding. "Are you kidding? Is she going to go postal on us? Oh my god, this is serious."

I could see it now.

Former kindergarten teacher on her way to LA, stops over in Denver for a short stay, only to be murdered by a coworker at the Tableau Club...

What a fine end that would be.

"We're just... careful. Let's put it that way," he said.

Um yeah. And that woman was just crazy.

"Is she obsessed with Maze? She warned me to stay away from him. What a weird thing to say."

He nodded. "I know. She's whacked."

Robbie and I, now in close quarters wiping up

Psycho's mess, paused for a moment, just looking at each other.

I almost forgot I hated him.

And then Maze appeared. Instead of hiding from psycho, he grabbed a seat at the bar while the last few customers straggled out.

I looked between Robbie and him. How did two such beautiful men end up working in one place? Was it a prerequisite for owning a popular club?

You had to be a hot guy?

"Maze, have you met Stell?" Robbie asked, pointing at his partner.

I could feel a strong heat rush up my neck and over my face. Guess he didn't know about Marni's and my debut there the other night, getting close and personal with too many martinis.

Maze smirked. "Oh, yeah. I've met this young lady. She was in the other night with Marni. They made quite an impression. Hey, how'd you feel the next day, Stell?"

Robbie's eyes widened.

I shrugged. "Not bad, but I can't say the same for Marni."

Time to eat crow.

I put on my humble face. "Sorry we were such jerks, Maze. I don't actually remember much, but I'm sure we were horrible."

Psycho appeared, and shaking out her blonde hair, sidled up to Maze. "Hi," she said, leaning onto the bar with one elbow, trying to be casual.

He recoiled before he could stop himself. Wow. They *so* needed to get rid of that woman.

"Hey, Annabel," he muttered, angling slightly away from her.

I decided to help him out, and needle Robbie at the same time. "So Maze, did you know Robbie and I were already acquainted, before I showed up to work here?"

He looked between the two of us, still pretending Annabel wasn't breathing down his neck. "You guys know each other?" he asked, puzzled.

Robbie sighed and just kept stocking beer bottles. He knew what was coming

"Well. I wouldn't say we *know* each other. But our paths have crossed. Or should I say our paths have *crashed*?"

Maze's eyes widened. "Did you have something to do with his car accident last week?"

I burst out laughing. "It's more like *he* had something to do with *my* car accident last week. Your buddy here smashed into the back of my car, his insurance company is trying not to pay, and my journey to LA is indefinitely on hold."

"No fucking way," Maze said. "What a crazy coincidence. Robbie, sounds like you better get your shit together on this one."

He sent Maze a dirty look. "Don't get involved, man. It's complicated."

I scoffed. "Yeah. Paying for the damage you caused to someone's car is complicated. Really hard."

Dick. Now I was pissed all over again.

Time to go. I looked at my phone and saw my Uber pulling up.

"Hey, guys. Thank you all for a lovely first night as a barback."

I almost said bar bitch but stopped just in time. I needed this job, shitty as it was, for the time being.

I glanced over my shoulder before I headed out the door. Both Robbie and Maze were watching me, and Annabel was watching Maze, inching closer and closer to him.

Freak show.

When I got home, I dragged myself to my room and started running the tub water as hot as I could stand it while I poured half a bottle of Marni's expensive bubble bath in it. I peeled the clothes off my tired, sore body and sank into the water, hoping it would start healing me since I had to turn around and go right back to Tableau the next day.

As I soaked, I dove into one of my visualization exercises. LA might be fucked, but I wasn't giving up on going after what I wanted. I figured I had three goals in the short term: be indispensable at Tableau so I could keep making money for as long as I needed to, get my car fixed, and earn my yoga teacher training certificate. I closed my eyes and pictured each of these things until they seemed within my reach.

I wanted to add a fourth item—to get my ass the rest of the way to LA—but I was afraid to go that far. Like it was asking too much.

I had to take things in steps. Maybe that had been my mistake. It wasn't that LA was out of reach, it was just that I had to accomplish some things first. Like baby steps.

And stop thinking about how good looking Maze and Robbie were.

11

Cabot 'Cab' Hendricks

"MY FATHER'S being a dick again. But what else is new?"

I dropped my head into my hands. Bullshit was getting *old*.

Robbie, assigned to baby duty, jostled the little man to his other arm. "Hold up. He's asking for his money back? Like, *all* of his money back?" He glanced at Maze and sighed.

Yeah. It was that bad.

"I don't get it, Cab," Maze said, trying to make sense of the craziness that was my family. "He invests in Tableau, we build it to massive success—the biggest night club Denver has ever seen—and he wants to pull the plug? It doesn't make sense."

Welcome to the world of my father.

Jax squirmed in Robbie's arms, looked around my living room where we always met, and went right back to sleep. He was a cute little bastard. I hadn't been around babies much until Robbie knocked up the woman he was banging. I wasn't ready for one of my own, but it was nice to see my friend be a man and step up to the plate.

I continued. "As you know, Dad sent Marni and me out here to Denver to *sow our wild oats* as he put it. He set her up with the gym, and me with Tableau. He wanted us to see what we could do as entrepreneurs."

With a big cash infusion from him.

Robbie frowned. "What I don't get is why is he asking for his money back from you, but not Marni?"

The answer to that was probably the most distressing of all.

"He doesn't expect her to take over the family business like he does me. In his warped, sexist mind, he's giving her something to do before he marries her off and she starts squeezing out babies."

Maze dropped his head back and laughed. "I bet Marni takes really kindly to that way of thinking."

He wasn't kidding. My sister was a masterful businesswoman. She could probably run circles around Dad with the family business. But he didn't want her.

He wanted me.

Which was a problem.

I had no intention of leaving either Denver or the club.

That left me—and the guys, really—no choice but to find a way to pay Dad back. Get him out of our hair and out of our business.

"So, he actually said pay him back or he'll sell the club right out from under us? How can he do that?" Robbie asked.

"Dude, you know he's listed as the majority owner. We had to do that to get him to front us the money."

Maze rose and began pacing, running his fingers through his hair. I'd seen that before. The man was troubled.

I was too.

Robbie, Maze, and I had put every last bit of our blood, sweat, and tears into Tableau. The last few nights running up to its opening, we'd actually slept at the club on bench cushions so we didn't have to stop working on its build-out, which we mostly did ourselves in order to save money. Our dedication had paid off in spades.

Which I suspected was part of why Dad was being such a dick. He was jealous. He'd sent me to Denver to *teach me a lesson*, and show me how tough the world of business was. He'd never counted on my being successful.

"It's his passive-aggressive way of forcing me back to Philly to work for him."

Robbie shook his head. "So, he doesn't care about Maze or me, or how hard we've worked to make Tableau a success?"

I didn't answer. It wasn't necessary.

"All right. We'll just raise the money to pay him back. Let's book more parties in the Playroom. We make a shit ton of money from that. And we can bump up the cover charge. We can also start being open on Mondays. Even though it won't be busy, that could provide some revenue we aren't currently getting," Maze said.

Robbie leaned back on my sofa and Jax snuggled into his neck. "Man, that's our only day off all week. Shit. But if we have to do it, I guess we have to do it." He closed his eyes and for a moment I thought he'd fallen asleep.

I didn't know anything about babies, but I could see via Robbie's recent experience that they seemed to sleep when they felt like it, and to hell with the rest of the world.

"We'll go over the numbers with Deb. She's great at that shit," Maze said. "Hey, did Robbie tell you about the new barback named Stell?"

Stell? Did I know someone named Stell?

Robbie's head popped up off the sofa back. "Piece of work, that one," he said.

Maze slapped his thigh. "Not only did she come in with no idea of what a barback did, but she also realized, the moment she arrived, that Robbie was the guy who hit her car last week. And now his insurance is trying to get out of paying for it." He smacked his thigh and started laughing his ass off.

Robbie didn't think it was funny.

"What a mess," I said.

"It will all get straightened out. She just needs to be patient," Robbie said. "What I *can* tell you is that I can't remember the last time I saw a more beautiful woman."

There was no shortage of beautiful women in our lives, thanks to Tableau. When you were owner of a popular club, women swarmed around you like flies on shit. Maze and I had accepted our newfound celebrity with caution. In fact, that was pretty much how Maze ended up being voted Denver's Most Eligible Bachelor.

Robbie, however, hadn't taken all the attention in stride and instead dove into the middle of it. And that's pretty much how he ended up a baby daddy.

So, for him to call out this woman as exceptional— well, she must be pretty special. Not that any of us had much time or energy for women. We had some pretty big fish to fry.

"Beautiful or not," Robbie said shrugging, "I doubt she'll be back. She was hating on the shit work."

Understandable.

Maze looked at his watch. "Okay guys, thanks for the meeting. I want to get over to the club. You wanna ride with me, Cab?"

"Let's do it."

We looked at Robbie. "I have to bring Jax to Elise's mom. Grandmas always be babysitting."

Ugh. Another reminder to keep my dick in my pants.

Cab

WE WERE GEARING up for a busy night where both Maze and I would be working the main bar.

"Fuck, there's Annabel," he said under his breath.

She walked around setting up tables, all while continually looking in his direction.

"When are you getting rid of her, man? Just let me do it," I whispered.

"You know her father's an investor here. It's not that easy."

Seemed like investments never came without big, ugly strings attached to them.

I shook my head as I wiped down our liquor bottles

and looked around. Where was our barback? I didn't need to be wasting my time cleaning shit.

"Hi, Maze. How are you today?" a voice behind me sang.

"Hey, Stell, good to see you. Hope you're ready for a busy night," he said.

Thank goodness. The barback was here. I turned to meet her, curious about her supposed great looks, and wondering what the hell she was doing accepting such a dirty job.

Oh.

Shit.

There was a churning in my stomach and for a moment I tasted bile.

No, no, no.

I swallowed hard so I wouldn't get sick. "Estella? Estella, is that you?" I stammered.

This was our new barback?

What the fuck?

Maze looked between the two of us and fake-smacked his head. "Of course! You guys already know each other. Stell is Marni's friend. For Christ's sake, you all grew up together, didn't you? I completely forgot to put that together." He beamed at the small world-ness of it all.

I glared at him.

Yeah, he'd completely forgotten.

And my sister Marni had completely forgotten, too.

But he was oblivious, clearly delighted that a 'friend of the family' had joined the team.

"My name is *Stell* now," the former Estella said in a flat voice.

Maze continued stacking glasses, happily reciting a rap song to himself.

She did not look happy. "Yeah, um, Marni neglected to mention that you worked here, too."

"So funny," Maze added in between his humming.

Holy shit. Estella Kline. Here. In Denver. At Tableau.

And we were going to be working together.

"Hey, guys, can you excuse me for a sec? I gotta run to the men's room." I casually walked away, and the second I was around the corner, I grabbed my cell and dialed Marni.

"Hey, Cab," she said cheerfully.

I wanted to kill her. Maze didn't know about my history with this woman, but my sister sure as hell did.

"Marn. Why didn't you tell me Estella Kline was coming to work at the club? Actually, why didn't you tell me she was coming to Denver?" I hissed.

"Cripes, bro. Calm down. I guess I just didn't think about it."

She was so full of shit.

"I don't appreciate this, Marn. And I suspect your friend Estella does not, either."

"Oh, Cab, she goes by Stell now. Estella just didn't suit her personality—"

"I'm pissed, Marn. You should have told me."

Weights clanked in the background. She was clearly making her rounds, like she did a hundred times a day. "Look, Cab, don't be upset with me. Talk to your damn business partners. I mean, don't you guys tell each other anything? Jesus."

"They told me someone named Stell had come to work for us, who, by the way, was a big pain in the ass. But they didn't tell me Estella Kline from Philadelphia, Pennsylvania, whose dad is a congressman, and who we grown up with, was coming to join us. And, who I just happened to—"

One of her staff was talking to her in the background. "Cab, I gotta go. Sorry."

And she was gone.

Goddammit.

I leaned against the wall and closed my eyes. This wasn't good. Not at all.

I returned to the bar to find Stell polishing the glasses she'd just taken out of the steaming dishwasher. She studiously avoided my gaze.

I cornered Maze. "Dude. This is not going to work for me," I whispered.

He looked at me, confusion all over his face. "Really? You don't want to work with someone from home?"

I couldn't even answer that.

He leaned closer. "Don't worry, man. She won't last

longer than a couple days, anyway. She's miserable. Look at her. Natural attrition."

Okay, that didn't really help. And the club was filling quickly. I needed to get working.

A bachelorette party group made their way to the bar.

"Hey, mister," one of them called. "Who's Denver's Most Eligible Bachelor? Is it you?" she asked, pointing my way.

I shook my head. "Sorry, ladies. It's that handsome fellow over there, Maze Abbot."

They looked at each other and broke into giggles. "Hi, Maze," the one wearing a 'Kiss Me, I'm the Bride' sash hollered.

Maze glared at me.

"What can I get you ladies?" I asked, guessing they'd go for Cosmos or Sex on the Beach shooters.

They looked at each other, letting the bride-to-be speak for them. "We want margaritas, please."

Cool. That was easy enough, especially since I was distracted by Estella/Stell slamming things around the bar.

Once a hot head, always a hot head.

"But," the bride called, "we'd like frozen. I want blueberry."

"I'll take mango."

"I'll take regular lime. No salt, though."

"I'll take creamsicle.

"And I'll take…. strawberry."

They looked at each other, thrilled with their choices. "Yay. This way we can all try each other's," one of them gushed.

Great. Everyone wanted something different. I was going to kill whoever added those stupid fruity margaritas to our drink menu. This was going to take me a fucking half hour.

"Have fun, buddy," Maze teased, elbowing me in the ribs.

Thanks, pal.

"And hurry, Mister Bartender. We're thirsty," the bride ordered.

Jesus. I wondered how many of these things she and her posse would consume before the night was out.

I pulled out the frozen fruit and started pouring shit into blenders.

"Estella?" I said.

"It's *Stell*," she hissed, not looking at me.

"Sorry. Stell. Have they shown you yet how to ring up a sale?"

She glared at me. I was getting lots of glares lately.

"Yes."

"Great. Can you ring up this order and get one of their credit cards? Those girls are here for the long haul and will be running up a hefty bill."

"Yes," she said, heading over to them.

"Ladies, whose credit card shall we use for this?" I heard her asking.

"Here. Take mine."

"No, no, no. This is my treat. Here, take mine," another said.

The bride leaned over the bar toward Stell. "Hey, that cute bartender there, the one with the dimples?"

I was the only one with dimples. I kept my head down and focused on my frozen drinks.

"What about him?" Stell asked.

"Is he single?"

I turned to find them all looking at me, and Stell rolling her eyes.

"I have no idea. Why don't you ask him," she said, taking the card to the register.

I switched on the blender so the customers couldn't hear us. "Um, you could help a guy out, you know? Tell them I'm married or something?"

Stell stopped what she was doing and looked up at me. In her sneakers, she seemed so small. And her eyes were as captivating as they'd always been.

"Sure, Cab. I'll tell them that. I'll also tell them that if there's a virgin in the group, you'll be happy to fuck her and then leave town, never to be heard from again."

13

Stell

"YOU'RE HOME EARLY! How was your second day on the job?"

I sank into the opposite end of the sofa where Marni sat, kicked my shoes off, and folded my feet under myself.

Should I tell her and then kill her? Or skip straight to the killing part?

"Um, Marn. You neglected to tell me your brother was part of the crew at Tableau."

She kept clicking TV channels, avoiding my gaze. "Oh. Did I?"

There was no way she 'forgot' to tell me.

"You know you did."

She finally looked at me and shrugged, tucking her black hair neatly behind her ears. "So what's the big deal?"

Was she really asking me that?

"You know what the big deal is." I reached forward and snatched the remote out of her hands.

"Hey!"

I gave her the best stink eye I could muster. It was hard to stay mad at her. We went back too far and had too much history.

She rolled her eyes. "Okay, okay. I knew you wouldn't go if you knew, but I thought if you saw him there and realized it wasn't going to be so bad, you could deal. You need the work, right?"

Yeah, I did need the work, especially since she'd fired me from her gym. But I'd promised myself I wouldn't bring that up again.

I hadn't seen Cab in years. I knew he and Marni had moved to Denver together, just to give it a try, and that their dad had even rented them an apartment to share in the beginning. But when Marni's gym took off, she got her own place. I'd lost track of what Cab was doing. I never asked. I didn't want to know.

And dammit, he still had those dimples. The ones that had bewitched me ever since Marni and I were little girls, when we would spy on him and his friends building forts and go-carts.

Yeah, I'd pretty much had a mad crush on him all my life. In the early years I couldn't even speak in his presence, that's how he affected me. I'd tried to hide it, and while most people were thankfully oblivious, Marni knew. And she kept my secret like the good friend that she was.

"So, how was it?" she asked with a slight flinch.

Jesus. Did she think I was going to hit her?

"I don't know who was more shocked, Cab or me. But it wasn't fun or fun*ny*, Marni. You know how he broke my heart."

Picking at her manicure, she was quiet. "I'm sorry. That wasn't cool. I guess I hadn't thought it all the way through."

"Well anyway, those customers sure throw themselves at the bartenders. I don't get it. Sure, the guys are good looking and all, but they're kind of douche-y stuck on themselves types. They make drinks. Big fucking deal. What's so impressive about that?"

I was on a roll.

Marni shook her head. "There's more to it than that. They're the face of the club. They're like the hosts who make sure people have a good time and that they come back."

How many of those women went home with the guys? Actually, I didn't want to know.

Since I had the remote, I started surfing. I considered a shark thriller, but I knew they scared the shit out of Marni. She'd not been in the ocean since we saw *Jaws* as kids.

"I'm going to call home," I said, unfolding myself

from the sofa. "Haven't checked in in a while." I tossed her the remote.

"Hi, Mom," I said, putting my cell phone on *speaker* once I'd closed the door to my bedroom.

"Estella, sweetie. Are you still in Denver?" she asked.

I plopped onto my bed. "Yup. Everything is great. I'm just taking a little break from driving so I can spend some time with Marni," I lied.

They didn't need to know the ugly truth about what was going down in my life.

Crashed car. Shit job. Offered a position as an escort. Bad reunion with old flame.

Thank you sir, may I have another?

"Oh, wonderful," she said. "Maybe while you're there you can see her brother, too."

Was I the only person who hadn't been aware Cab was still in Denver?

"Is Dad there?" I asked to change the subject.

"He just walked in. You timed it perfectly."

Not really. I knew exactly when he got in on Thursday nights after having taken the train from DC. He traveled home to Philly every Thursday night and went back to DC, at least when Congress was in session, every Sunday night.

"Estella? Are you there?" Dad said loudly into the speakerphone Mom had switched us to.

"Hi, Dad. How was the train?"

"Wonderful. I think everyone should travel by train," he boomed.

"How are things looking for the reelection?" I ventured.

This was a sensitive topic. When I'd bailed on marrying Vaughn one week before the wedding, you'd think my parents might have been pissed about all the money they were out of. I mean, they *were* pissed about that, for sure, but of utmost importance to them was how it would make them *look*.

Turned out a daughter flaking on her wedding was not 'good optics,' as Dad's campaign manager had said.

Why didn't *he* marry Vaughn, then?

After the announcement came out, the press had descended on my parents' house like there'd been a murder. It was completely ridiculous. And when they found out I'd moved out of my townhouse with Vaughn, and back home with them, they started following me everywhere to see if I had another man.

That's when I decided to flee to LA.

"Um, sweetie, we were wondering if you'd had any contact with Vaughn," Mom said breezily.

I knew they were going to go there. I just knew it.

"Mom, I told you, I'm through with him. It's over. There's no reason to talk to him."

I could see them now, looking at each other and frowning, trying to figure out how to talk some sense into me.

"Well, Estella, that doesn't mean you won't reconsider your decision someday. I just hope you don't end up regretting this," Dad said.

Did they want me to be with a cheating scumbag?

My mother cleared her throat. "Why, honey, I saw Vaughn at the grocery store just the other day. He looked so sad."

He was sad he wouldn't have a high-ranking congressman as his father-in-law. Not because he missed me.

"He asked where you were staying."

Oh no. She didn't.

"Mom, please tell me you didn't tell him—"

"I did, Estella. He's so bereft. He deserves the chance to change your mind."

Oh no, no, no.

"Is he coming here? To Denver?"

There was a brief silence, and then someone drew a long breath.

"He might be."

Fuck, fuck, fuck.

How many times had I told my parents to tell Vaughn nothing about what I was doing or where I was?

"It sounds like I need to stop sharing my whereabouts with you guys, if you're going to share them with the very person I asked you not to," I snapped.

There was an icy silence.

"Young lady, your mother and I don't appreciate being spoken to that way. Now, my election is heating up and we are facing a world of hurt—"

This is where I tuned him out. *World of hurt* was his

favorite saying. He used it all the time, whether at home or on the floor of the House of Representatives.

"Hey, guys, I just realized how late it is there on the East Coast. I'd better let you go. Talk to you soon," I said.

"Bye, honey," Mom said.

"Goodbye, Estella. We love you," Dad said.

"Love you too," I said and swiped my phone closed.

Just what I needed on top of the other stuff going on in my life. Vaughn showing up in town. That was going to be one shit show I didn't want to see.

14

Stell

"ARE you *sure* we should be doing this?"

Marni grabbed my free hand. My other one was busy adjusting the wig she'd made me wear.

"Would you come on? They'll never know it's us."

Tableau was having some sort of private masked party, and Marni and I had specifically been told we were *not* invited.

Which meant, of course, that we were going to do our damnedest to go.

Thus, the wigs, over the top stage makeup, and costumes from Marni's Burning Man days.

She was right. The guys would never recognize us. But that didn't make me feel any better about crashing.

We walked toward the club's front door with our heads down, just in case.

"Wait." I grabbed her arm. "Stop. Marn, they're checking the invite list at the front door." I turned to head back to the car.

But she still had hold of my hand.

"Stell," she hissed. "Goddammit, c'mon. You think I don't know how to sneak into my brother's club? Now, stay close," she scolded, yanking on my hand again.

We walked to the back of the club to a door that had a pad with numbered buttons.

She pressed a series of numbers, and the light on the lock stayed red. She tried another series. No luck.

"Can we leave now?" I whispered.

But the last series she entered turned the light green, and the door popped open enough for us to slip in.

"Victory," she said, slipping inside after me.

"Oh my god. How did you know the code?" I asked.

"They always use one of their birthdays. So dumb."

We scooted through bar's backroom and emerged into a party in full swing.

"Act like you belong here," she said with her brilliant smile and started weaving through the costumed crowd.

"Here, put one of these masks on."

I pulled a black velvet mask over my face until the eye holes lined up, and fixed the elastic around the back of my silver wig.

As we wandered, I got more comfortable with my costume. Marni had been right. No one would recognize us. It felt great.

I could get used to being someone else from time to time.

"C'mon. Let's go upstairs," she said over the booming house music.

We grabbed fresh glasses of champagne off the bar and mounted the stairs to the club's mezzanine, where the private party rooms were.

I'd only seen the mezzanine once, when I was checking the place out. There were sofas and chairs overlooking the floor below, and a couple smaller rooms for private parties. One was called the Playroom.

I could just imagine.

"Hey. Do I know you?"

I looked up right at Maze.

Oh shit, oh shit, oh shit.

Marni looked down and slunk away.

Thanks, pal.

"I don't think so," I said, sipping my champagne and avoiding his eyes.

"I'm digging that silver wig. You have this Cleopatra thing going on," he said, nodding. "Hey, you're almost done with that champagne. Let me get you another one."

Oh my god. Now was my chance.

I had no idea where Marni had disappeared to, but I

started toward the stairs as soon as Maze turned his back to me.

But I wasn't fast enough.

"Hey, where are you going? Here's your champagne," he said, handing it to me.

I took a big swig. "Oh. Great. Thank you."

He stared for an awkward moment, then smiled. "I'm going to go mingle for a bit. Enjoy yourself," he said, twirling a piece of silver wig material between his fingers.

Holy shit. I didn't need my freaking boss to be flirting with me, no matter how hot he was. Attraction to him was not in the cards for me.

No way. That would just be so irresponsible. I couldn't.

Could I?

Oh, what the fuck.

I found him not ten feet away, talking to some guy.

"Oh, and here comes the silver Cleopatra," he said as I approached, his wicked grin weakening my knees.

I should just get out of there immediately. Like right away.

But I didn't.

I raised my champagne glass to him. "Thank you again. This is very yummy."

He took a step closer to me, and his friend drifted away. "I think you're very yummy."

I tilted my head and smiled, emboldened by the second glass of bubbles. He smelled so good.

"I'm Maze. What's *your* name?" he asked.

"Cleo. I'm Cleo tonight," I said, thinking fast.

He leaned next to my ear and kissed it.

Holy shit. Maze just kissed me.

And it was freaking hot.

Oh, what the hell.

I turned toward him until our lips brushed lightly, and I licked my lips. He tasted good, like smooth, expensive scotch and something minty.

When he put a hand on the back of my neck, there was no turning back. He gently pulled me toward him, as if he were trying to assess my interest, and kissed me with slightly parted lips.

I put my hands on the sides of his gorgeous face, gazing directly into his amazing blue eyes, and kissed him back.

"Wow," he said, shaking his head as if to get rid of the cobwebs. "Just wow."

He took one of my hands, snapping me out of my trance.

Oh boy. I'd just kissed my boss. He was going to figure out it was me underneath the wig, makeup, and crazy clothes, and fire my ass.

I'd already been fired once in Denver, and I'd only been there a few days.

I wanted to keep kissing him. I really did.

But I wanted my job more.

Time to wrap this shit up.

"Um, Maze, a cab is waiting for me downstairs," I lied. "I gotta get going."

I pulled my hand out of his and literally ran down the stairs, through the club, and out the front door where guests were still arriving, with no idea where Marni was. I still had my champagne glass so I left it on the ground beside the door. A taxi had just started pulling away after dropping off a carload of people, and I knocked on the window just in time.

"Oh my gosh. Am I glad to see you," I said breathlessly, jumping in the backseat.

"Where to, ma'am?" he asked.

I looked out the back window to make sure Maze hadn't followed me, and sure enough, he dashed out the front door, looking in every direction.

I sank low in my seat, sad I'd bailed on him. He was sexy, and hot, and nice, and thought my outfit was cool... and his kiss... Wow. Just wow.

"Ma'am?" the driver repeated. "Where to?"

"Sorry. Anywhere but here."

15

Maze

The silver-haired Cleopatra.

I couldn't get her out of my mind.

Beautiful women streamed through Tableau all day, every day. And while I usually kept my dick in my pants, many of them were pretty eager to... well, get to know us guys. But we were learning the hard way it was best not to mix business and pleasure—whether with customers or employees.

I'd made the mistake once of letting Annabel talk me into going out to dinner, finishing the night with a chaste kiss. Two years later, she still thought we had something going on and her behavior was becoming increasingly erratic. Cab and Robbie wanted me to just fire her ass, but knowing how whacko she was, I hesitated to take action. On top of that, we were indebted —literally—to her old man. But something had to be done.

Resting my elbows on the office desk, I put my head in my hands. I felt a huge weight on my back, and it was getting heavier every day.

Not to mention, Cab's father's putting the screws to him. Well, us really. If he wanted his quarter million bucks back, it was everybody's problem, not just Cab's.

But if last night's private party was any indication of our ability to raise quick cash, repaying Mr. Hendricks was within the realm of possibility.

A quick look at the numbers showed we'd made a sweet ten grand. If we got aggressive about scheduling these babies, we could pay him back in less than a year.

Question was, did we have that long before he pulled the plug?

A knock on the office door startled me, and when I opened my eyes again, a couple pieces of glitter had fallen onto the desk below me. Where had that come from? I ran my fingers through my hair, and more floated out, like the white stuff in a snow globe.

Goddammit. Every single time we had a party I somehow got glitter in my hair. It was like it got into the air filtration system.

I brushed a hand over my paperwork and pushed the glitter into a trashcan.

"Come in."

The door opened slowly.

"Hey, Stell."

"Oh, hi, Maze. Didn't know you'd be up here. I wanted to check the schedule."

I pointed behind me with my thumb. "It's up there on the wall."

She slipped behind my chair in the tight office and began typing this week's schedule into her phone.

"What is that I smell?" I asked, turning around. It seemed so familiar.

And was that a piece of something silver in Stell's hair?

She turned around carefully, pretty much wedged between the wall and the back of my office chair. "My perfume, I guess. Hope it doesn't bother you. I don't wear much anymore because so many people are allergic and stuff. But I figured it would be good to wear here when I started to sweat." She giggled nervously.

Why was she nervous?

I stood, careful not to squash her into the wall. "What's that in your hair?" I asked, plucking at a piece of silver tinsel.

Her eyes widened. "Oh. Hmmm. Look at that. Must have picked it up in the gym." She shrugged, snatching it from my fingers and stuffing it into her jeans pocket.

She backed against the wall to squeeze out of the office, her gaze glued to mine the whole time.

What was it about this woman?

She suddenly broke into a smile. "Hey, you have a piece of glitter on your forehead."

"Oh. Shit," I said, rubbing my face.

She shook her head. "No, you missed it. It's right… there," she said, pointing.

I kept rubbing. Fuck this glitter shit.

"Wait, I think I can get it," she said, reached a finger toward me and giving me a little *flick*.

"There it is. See?" she said, holding out a finger with one tiny square of the shiny crap.

We both stared at the offender.

"I didn't take you for the glitter type," she said, her smile turned up at one corner.

It was getting warm in the office. Very warm.

"I'm not. There was a costume party here last night. People go crazy with glitter these days."

Her eyebrows rose. "Oh. That's right. There was a private party. How'd it go?" she asked curiously.

"It was really good. Very profitable. We need to have a lot more of them."

She looked at her watch. "Well, I'm on now. Gotta get back downstairs. But if you ever need me to work one of those parties, let me know."

I wasn't sure about that. But it was nice of her to offer. Some of our private parties got pretty fucking crazy.

"Thanks. I'll do that."

Just before she left the office, I spotted another strand of silver stuff tangled in her hair.

16

Maze

IT WASN'T my day to tend bar, and since I'd gone over the previous night's receipts, I could theoretically go home. But I didn't.

Instead, I found myself heading downstairs, pretending to check out the tables and chairs on the main floor, as if I were looking for something. But what I was really doing was looking at Stell. Every chance I could get.

Dammit.

I had to hand it to her. Barback was a shit job, but she mastered it like a champ. At first, she was a handful with a shitty attitude, but she quickly hit her stride. Now she stayed in perpetual motion, always finding one thing or the other to clean, restock, or organize. She could fetch a full keg from the cooler in about a minute flat, and have it perfectly hooked up in another minute.

Male barbacks who'd worked here for ages couldn't do anything that fast.

And she was cute as shit when testing the first pour of a new keg, pulling the tap all the way forward, tilting her glass at a perfect angle. She even bit her bottom lip while she did it, assessing the ratio of bubbles to beer to make sure the level of gas going into the keg was just right.

She looked like a damn scientist running an experiment.

Like the scumbag that I was, I moved from the tables where I was pretending to look for something, to a seat at the end of the bar. It was still just late afternoon, and we had just a few patrons trickling in. I sat and scrolled through my phone.

And of course, watched the lovely Stell.

As the dishwasher finished its latest cycle, Stell pulled it open and let the steam waft away before she dove in. Then, she picked up the rack of glasses and set them on top of the shelf behind the bar to start polishing.

But before she started that, she took a rag and actually wiped out the dishwasher.

Who did that?

I mean, we were supposed to do that to keep the thing working in top condition. But nobody ever did.

Jesus. She was meticulous.

And when she bent over to wipe the last of the water, a lacy black thong revealed itself as her jeans slipped down on her ass.

Her lovely ass.

She self-consciously pulled her work T-shirt down and tucked it into the back of her jeans, and as she stood, she turned and caught me staring.

Busted.

She waved, oblivious to my shameless staring. "Hey, Maze. Didn't know you were sticking around."

I stretched and looked at my watch as if I had somewhere important to go. "Yeah. I gotta hit the road in a bit."

She walked over and leaned on the bar in front of me. I had to force myself not to look at the tiny swath of black lace bra peeking out of her shirt.

I wanted to know more about her.

"Hey, Stell. Why are you working as a barback anyway?"

I had to ask. For one, I felt like a shit for making it hard for her in the beginning, having assumed she'd naturally bail on the backbreaking work. But not only did she not run away screaming, she took the work up a notch, completing everything she had to do and then some.

She pressed her lips together as resignation flashed across her face. "You really want to know?"

"Only if it's a seriously juicy story," I laughed.

She raised her eyebrows. "Some might say so. That's for sure."

I looked at her, and waited. Was she going to tell me? I *knew* she had a story. Girls like her did not take shit jobs like this. There was definitely something up.

"I was supposed to get married," she paused to look at her watch, "exactly two weeks ago today."

She pressed her lips together.

"Damn. Did he leave you at the altar?"

Her head snapped back and she frowned. I got the express impression I'd just put my foot in my mouth.

She pulled her shoulders back and raised her chin. "No. I left *him*."

Oh, damn. The volcano was about to erupt. And I was right in its path.

She slammed a heavy rocks glass down on the bar. The thud it made was so loud that several people turned in our direction.

She pointed a finger at me. "*Why* is it that people assume it's the woman who gets left by the man? Do they think we have no agency at all? No brains?"

To emphasize the fact, she pointed at her head. "Well, you know what? Women walk away, too. *All the time*," she spat, getting right in my face.

"Jesus," she hissed, walking away with big, stomping steps.

Guess I blew that one.

Okay. So she bailed on her wedding. That takes balls, for sure. And I respected that, even though I wasn't any closer to an explanation of how she came to take the job at Tableau. But at least I had a little insight into the drama in her life. She'd made a change—a big change—and had clearly left town without the funds to sustain herself. It wasn't hard to put those things together.

And Robbie had done a number on her car, to further complicate things.

I wondered, could I help her somehow? She deserved it, facing a tough situation and making the best of it without complaining. Another woman might bellyache all day long, waiting for someone to save her.

I texted the guys that I wanted to find a way to help her. They might think I was crazy, but as hard as she was working for us, it was the least we could do.

And her being hot as shit, wearing little lacy thongs, had nothing to do with it.

At all.

Seriously.

Maybe she was interested in tending bar. She'd make more money, that was for sure. She had a tendency to blow up over small things but if she could learn to bite her tongue and handle difficult situations, she might be a good addition to my bartending school. And a new session was starting soon. I made a mental note to bring it up to her once she'd gotten over my latest insult—*if* she ever got over it.

As I sneaked glimpses of her working, I watched her wipe a bead of sweat off her temple with the back of her hand. And as she did, I could swear I saw another piece of silver in her hair. Funny. She'd said she'd gotten it in her hair at the gym, but I think we both knew that was bullshit.

But I did know, because it was high time to be honest with myself, that I was looking for ways to keep her around. It might not be wise, but it sure would be nice.

For us both.

17

Stell

THOSE GUYS, the hotshot owners of Tableau, didn't know what a clean bar looked like before I came along and showed them.

Give me a male barback who could keep his work area so clean you couldn't smell stale beer if it was poured over your head.

Because that would never happen.

No guy would ever do half the shit I did to keep this bar in such great shape.

And did anyone notice it?

Acknowledge it?

Thank me?

Hell no.

Because, of course.

Men just don't see shit like that. At least none of the ones I'd ever known.

Unappreciated as I might have been, there was a serious upside to being a barback that I had not anticipated—it paid well. Who would have thought?

Sure, my hourly pay was something a couple pennies above minimum wage, but at the end of each night, the bartenders shared their tips with me. And on more than one occasion, I was pretty sure they were being a little more generous than they might have been with a guy. I wasn't complaining though, sexist as it might sound. I needed the damn money.

Last night when I'd gotten home, I counted up the cash I had stuffed in a sock at Marni's, and was thrilled to find that in a couple weeks' time I'd collected nearly two thousand dollars. 'Course I'd worked my ass off for that, but it felt damn empowering that I could raise money when I was in a bind, especially since Robbie the Wrecker's insurance still hadn't come through, and I was beginning to wonder if it ever would.

I mailed checks to pay my car registration and the ticket for blowing it off. *That* hurt.

Now to bail my car out of mechanic's jail.

One problem though. I wasn't ready to leave Denver.

The call of LA had gotten quieter in recent days. Maybe that's why I was developing a fondness for the mile-high city.

I took an Uber to the mechanic, who rolled his eyes when I counted out the cash I owed him in wrinkled fives, tens, and twenties.

Too bad. He hadn't done anything to make my life easier, having been unwilling to even start work on my car until he knew payment was forthcoming.

Regardless, he'd done a good job. My car looked great. Not like new, because it was about ten years old, but the evidence of Robbie's damage was gone, as if it had never happened. I got behind the wheel of my trusty little Toyota, cranked up Beyoncé, and drove away, wracking my brains for a plan.

I'd said I'd leave Denver when my car was fixed. Only, now I didn't want to.

Could I pretend my car was still in the shop?

How the hell would that work? It wasn't easy to hide a car.

Or was it?

I drove straight to Marni's and found a spot in the far back of the parking lot where people rarely left their cars because of the leaves and other crap the overhanging trees dropped. That might just work.

It was a little dishonest to not tell her my car was out of the shop. Maybe a lot dishonest. But I eventually would. I just wanted a few days to think through my next steps and develop a new plan.

Because I loved a plan.

I'd ask her if I could hang around long enough to take the yoga teacher training at Altitude. And if I kept working my butt off like I had been, I could even offer her some money for rent. Not that she'd take it.

I'd do anything to keep from having to ask my parents for money, that was for certain. Everything with them came at a price, and with Dad's reelection looming, god only knew what they'd expect of me.

After I'd successfully 'hidden' my car, it was time to get ready for work. It was going to be a busy night, and I was looking forward to making good money. I'd bought special insoles for my sneakers to cushion my feet. I was good to go.

I let myself into Marni's apartment, stopping for a moment once inside to take a deep inhalation. It always smelled so good there, partly because of the roses she kept in vases, and partly from the yummy lotions and reed diffuser air fresheners she bought from the local fancy pharmacy.

I grabbed my work shirt from the dryer—the black logo'd polo shirt that all the Tableau employees wore— and went back to my room to put on a little makeup. Just as I was changing, I heard water splash.

It had come from my bathroom.

Oh no. Was there a leak? Had the toilet overflowed?

Ugh. I knew nothing about plumbing.

Or was there an intruder?

An intruder who splashed water?

I looked at the door. I could easily run.

But I was mad at the world, and ready for a fight.

My heart started to pound. I looked around for

some sort of weapon and only came up with the heavy glass bowl that sat on my dresser. It would have to do. I hoisted it over my head, and tiptoed toward the bathroom.

I could do this.

When I was just outside the door, there was another small splash, followed by the sound of a man clearing his throat.

Oh my god. Was this the day I was going to die?

I screwed up my courage, ready to go on the big time offensive to take out whomever I had to.

Raising the heavy bowl over my head, I charged the bathroom.

"I'll kill you with this," I screamed, getting ready to swing.

"Wait. Please."

What the fucking fuck?

There was a man in my bathtub, his arms raised over his head in a defensive posture.

"Vaughn? Is that you? WHAT THE HELL ARE YOU DOING HERE?"

He peeked up at me, where he sat surrounded by bubbles.

"Don't hit me. Please," he winced.

I continued to hold the bowl up in the air. I didn't care that he wasn't an intruder, per se. I still didn't want him there, and it would have been within my rights to smash him over the head.

At least I thought so.

"WHAT ARE YOU DOING HERE?" I screamed.

"Gimmee the bowl, Stell. Here. Hand it to me," he said, his wet arms reaching for it.

"No! You get out of that goddamn tub, and out of this apartment now."

He stood up, the water riveting down his hairy naked body.

Did I really used to sleep with this guy? Ew.

Stepping out, he reached for a towel and wrapped it around his midsection, dripping water all over the place, just like he had when we'd lived together.

"Calm down, Stell," he said, holding his hands up like a criminal.

"How did you get in here?" I snapped.

"Marni. Marni let me in," he said, continuing to shrink away from the bowl in my swinging arm.

Marni? *She* knew he was here? And she let him in our fucking home? Oh, she was going to hear about this.

I suddenly didn't feel so badly for misleading her about my car.

"Well, get the hell out," I yelled. "You are not welcome here."

He rushed past me into the bedroom and down the hall to Marni's second guest bedroom. Where his shit was scattered all over the place.

He'd really made himself at home. Fucker.

"Pick this shit up and get out."

He dropped his towel and began to dress. "Stell, I came all the way here from Philly to see you."

"Well, you just wasted your time because I have no interest in seeing you. So you can just get in your car and head back home."

He sat on the edge of the bed while he pulled on his shoes and socks. "I wanted to apologize to you, Stell. I made a mistake. A big one. Please don't make me regret it for the rest of my life."

"You should have thought of that before you fucked Suza. Now get out."

He sighed and began putting his things back in his duffle bag.

"You have a lot of nerve helping yourself to a bath in Marni's apartment. In *my* bathroom."

"Yours was the only bathroom with a tub. And that bubble bath smelled so good." He smiled, thinking he could wear me down.

But I knew him, and I knew his tricks.

He kept trying. "Hey, you look good. You drop a couple pounds? And your hair looks much better now that it's getting longer."

Wow. Really?

Of course he was going to bring my weight and hair up. He'd always been borderline obsessed with both, trying to get me to shed some pounds and add some length.

"You have two minutes to get out before I call the cops."

He actually had the nerve to roll his eyes. "Go ahead. Marni let me in. I'm not trespassing."

"Vaughn, I left you because I didn't want to be with you. That means I don't want to see you either, and nothing you can say will change that. So get out."

He hoisted his bag onto his shoulder. "You know, Stell. I'm not going to wait for you forever to realize what a mistake you made. You humiliated me, your parents, and most of all, yourself."

I marched across the apartment and opened the front door. "Here you go, Vaughn. Goodbye. And do not return."

He pressed his lips together. "Fine. I'll go stay in a hotel. But I'm not leaving Denver without you."

"That's fine, Vaughn. Because I *will* be leaving Denver without you when I continue to LA." I gave him a shove, and closed the door in his face.

Shit, shit, shit.

I knew there'd be trouble once my mom had told him where I was. And I'm sure she couldn't give a shit that he'd stalked me more than halfway across the country. She wanted me to get back together with his sorry ass so badly she'd probably paid his damn way out here.

"Why did you let Vaughn in?" I demanded when Marni answered her phone.

She exhaled a long sigh. "Oh, Stell. He just showed up and he looked so sad. I mean, can't we all be friends? You know, handle this like mature adults?"

Oh. My. God.

She was rapidly working her way toward becoming my ex-best friend.

"No, Marn. Letting him in was not cool. Shit, my mother blabbing where I was hiding out wasn't cool either. Are you on my side or his?"

That would get her.

She sighed. "Okay. I get it. I'm sorry. I didn't see any harm."

"If he comes around again, we're calling the police."

She gasped. "Isn't that a bit… heavy handed?"

"Marni…" I warned.

"Okay. Okay," she said.

I sat down on one of the kitchen barstools, exhausted from fighting with both my ex-fiancé and best friend. I considered calling in sick to Tableau, that's how drained I was, but I didn't want to be another flaky employee. Besides, I wanted the money.

And the bartenders were pretty nice to look at.

Sadly, that was about the only thing working in my favor. I'd planned on life getting better when I left Philly. But apparently your shit follows you wherever you go.

18

Robbie

"Hey, do you have a sec?"

Stell looked over from scrubbing something behind the bar that had probably never been scrubbed in the whole history of Tableau. "What?" she asked, glaring at me.

Talk about holding a grudge.

She stood on one foot, hip jutting out, arms crossed, still holding her dirty rag.

I surveyed everything within her reach to make sure there were no sharp objects I needed to move.

"Stell, I wanted to say I'm sorry about the whole mess with your car."

Her eyebrows skeptically shot up.

"What are you saying, Robbie the Wrecker?" she asked, rolling her eyes.

"I got bad advice from my insurance company. I never should have let them run with the claim. They're major dicks."

"Takes one to know one."

She had a point there.

I stepped toward her, and she actually took a big step back. What the hell? Did she think I was dangerous?

"Stell, I can see you're a nice person. And I appreciate how hard you've been working for Tableau. This bar has never been so spick-and-span. I feel like calling the health inspectors just to show the place off."

I produced a small laugh.

She did not respond.

I reached into my pocket. "So, I'm just going to give you cash for the car repair. If insurance pays up, fine, but at least for now, you're whole." I placed a wad of hundreds in her hand.

"I hope three grand is enough. If it's not, please let me know. And again, I apologize for all the trouble I've caused you."

There, I'd done it. And it felt good.

Closed chapter.

But you'd think she'd just won the damn lottery.

She looked down at her open palm, holding thirty rolled up Benjamins wrapped with a thick rubber band.

"Uh…" She tried to speak, but nothing came out.

Damn. I knew she'd appreciate it but hadn't anticipated how much.

Guess I'd done a good thing.

"Uh…" she tried again. Her bottom lip quivered, followed by her upper lip. Then her whole mouth distorted and she covered her face with both hands.

"Oh my god," she wailed.

We caught the attention of only a couple customers, who smiled and returned to their drinks.

"Stell," I whispered. "Pull yourself together."

"You don't know what I've been going through," she wept. "It's… it's all been so haaard."

She looked up at me, her beautiful brown eyes bloodshot, her nose running. She hiccupped and reached for a napkin to wipe her nose, bawling for another five minutes while I rubbed her arm.

Sniffling, she cleared her throat and shook her shoulders. "Okay. I'm fine now. Thank you, Robbie. I'd be lying if I didn't say I am shocked. Completely."

Jesus, was I that big of an asshole?

"It's going to be all right, Stell."

That was the only thing I could think to say.

"Thank you, Robbie. I appreciate it. I'm sorry I didn't give you a chance to show you were a nice person earlier."

She had good reason not to.

The place was getting busy, and psycho Annabel waited at the end of the bar to pick up some drinks.

"Let's get back to work now, okay?"

"Just one more thing, Robbie," she said, taking a step toward me.

"What?"

"Can we keep this between us?" she asked quietly. "The money thing?"

"Um, sure, I guess. I wasn't going to broadcast it anyway."

She held up a finger. "Thanks. I don't want anyone to know you paid me. Then they'll expect me to continue on toward LA. And I don't want to leave Denver yet."

Is that all she wanted? Something about that news made me happy. Very happy.

"Well, I know we'd like for you to stay on as long as you can."

She smiled. She actually smiled. "So this can be our secret?"

Now that we were both in better moods, I was ready to try having a little fun.

I shrugged. "Depends. What's it worth to you?"

19

Robbie

WHAT A RELIEF it was to know that Stell no longer wanted to chop me into pieces. And even better, we worked in perfect unison all evening. I didn't have to ask her for a thing. She anticipated every need, and took care of things before I'd even noticed something needed to be done.

If only every barback could be like that. But I knew better. Like she'd told me, eventually, she'd hit the road and we'd be back to hiring mediocre slackers who half the time didn't bother showing up.

I glanced over at her, polishing glasses. She often hummed when she did, but for some reason she was staring into the crowd, frowning.

I followed her gaze to see what she was looking at.

Shit. Jax's baby momma was headed right for me at full speed.

"Here," she said, thrusting Jax at me over the bar. I set a glass and cocktail shaker down just in time to catch him.

What the?

There I was, behind the bar at Tableau, holding my baby.

Not only was that all kinds of inappropriate, it was also all kinds of illegal.

"Elise, what is going on?" I asked as Jax began to wail.

She stuck her chin out. "I'm going out with the girls tonight. You can watch Jax."

And she was gone.

Holy hell. She must have completely lost her marbles.

I looked around in a panic, half my customers wrinkling their noses in distaste and the other half cooing over a cute baby.

"Stell. Help," I called.

But she was already on her way over. "I've got him. I'll take him up to the office. Can you manage without me?"

Dear god, she was an angel. "Yes. Here's his diaper bag. Go. We can't have him behind the bar."

She threw the bag over her shoulder and pulled Jax close to her chest to try and block the bar's noise. She ran down to the end of the bar, lifted the hinged countertop, and took off up the stairs.

Jesus Christ. What had Elise been thinking?

And what had I been thinking the night I met her right here at the bar?

She'd come in with a group of friends, and even though they seemed to be having a good time, she'd stared at me pretty much the whole night. And when they left an hour later, she stayed behind. I was captivated, I couldn't lie.

Once again, I was thinking with my little head.

That's how I ended up with little Jax.

Not that I would change a thing. My boy was amazing beyond words. I did worry for him though, because the acrimony between his mother and I was pretty ugly. He was unaware of it now, of course, but the time would come where it would be all too evident that his parents couldn't stand each other. Not an ideal way to grow up.

I'd fully supported Elise's choice to have the baby, but I also made it clear from the get-go that it didn't mean we were going to be a couple. That made her unhappy. Very unhappy. And every decision she'd made since then was designed to punish me to the maximum extent possible.

I buzzed Stell up in the office. "Hey. Everything okay?"

She laughed and Jax cooed in the background like a

little bird. "We're having a ball. Don't worry about a thing."

"Okay. Do I need to come change his diaper or anything?"

"Nope," she said. "I already did."

Christ. I was going to owe this woman a lot more than three thousand dollars.

When the night was finally over and the crowd had thinned, I ran up to the office as fast as I could and blew the door open.

"Oh my god, Stell, I am so sorry—"

But I immediately shut up. Stell was sitting, propped up in a corner, asleep, with Jax on her chest, also asleep.

Holy shit. Where was my fucking camera?

I took a couple quick snaps and then walked over to the two of them, gently taking Jax out of her arms. The movement shook Stell awake, and she looked around the room confused. Then she looked at me, even more confused.

"Wha… what's going on?" she mumbled.

I extended a hand to help her to her feet.

"Stell, I think you are the world's best babysitter."

She rubbed her eyes and yawned. "Oh my god, I can't believe I fell asleep. I was holding Jax because I knew he was tired. I must have dozed off too."

Didn't think I'd ever see the woman whose car I wrecked napping with my baby.

I wrapped Jax in the baby blanket Elise had been

thoughtful enough to bring. He stirred, smacked his lips, and then went back to sleep.

God, how did I get so lucky?

"You must have a lot of experience with babies, Stell."

She shrugged. "Just from babysitting as a teenager."

I was amazed.

"I'll tell ya what," I said.

"Hmmm?"

"Your secret. Hiding the fact that you now have enough money to head to LA."

Her eyes widened. "Oh. What about it?"

I took a step toward her, Jax burrowed into my chest.

"If you let me kiss you, I'll promise to keep your secret."

She scrunched up her face, trying not to smile. "That's extortion."

Damn right it was.

I shifted Jax to one arm and pulled Stell to me with my free one, weaving my fingers through her hair and holding her head.

Our gazes locked for one second, and my mouth crashed into hers, the animosity between us forgotten, the tension unraveling.

"You are so beautiful," I breathed into her mouth.

My words came out jumbled but she knew exactly what I'd said. Her arms flew up around my neck, careful to miss Jax, and I kissed her like I'd wanted to since the day I hit her car.

20

Stell

I was not only now a big liar, but also a big ho bag.

I had the money and car to get my ass to LA but was pretending I didn't, and I'd just shared a passionate kiss with another one of the guys I worked with.

The only one left was Cab and, well, I'd kissed him a long time ago. No need to go through that again.

I could see it now. He'd be running his lips down the side of my neck, romantically holding my hand, and his eyes would open wide as he realized he had somewhere else to be.

Like another freaking state.

Yeah, I wasn't giving that shit bag another chance to run out on me. He could kiss my ass.

But the other guys, Robbie and Maze? Why not? Everybody else was having fun. Why shouldn't I? Besides, I'd be hitting the road eventually, so I didn't give a shit what they thought of me.

Well, sort of.

"Hey, Marn," I said, arriving at the gym.

She was at the front desk greeting members, like she usually was. She liked to provide what she called 'the personal touch'.

"Hey, Stell. You still mad at me? About Vaughn?" she asked cautiously.

Geez. Since I'd kissed Robbie, I'd almost forgotten about that scumbag.

I shrugged, to make her work for it. "Maybe a little."

She pursed her lips. "I was hoping we could all be friends. You know, like we used to be."

Really? She was going there?

I took a deep breath to summon my patience. "Maybe we all will be friends someday. Like look back at this and laugh a little. But that is a long way off because right now, I hope that asshole gets hit by a bus."

She studied me, possibly absorbing for the first time exactly how things had gone down between us.

It had been quite simple, really. A week before the wedding, some anonymous Good Samaritan had dropped off an envelope of photos at the townhouse we shared. Luckily, I'd gotten home before Vaughn, because it turned out he'd been watching for them and had planned to make an interception. But his plan failed, as did the fling he was having with one of my bridesmaids.

I don't know who took the photos, or delivered them to our house, but I will be eternally grateful.

I took them straight to my parents', knowing they'd resist cancelling the wedding without solid proof. When they got their first look at a photo of Vaughn out to dinner with my now-former friend, his arm draped around her shoulder with his hand slipped up her skirt, they didn't need to see any more.

I didn't show them the one of her sucking his dick. I'd been tempted, though.

They made a big deal about trying to *work it out*, as they put it. Mom lectured me that couples survive infidelity all the time, and that maybe Vaughn and I could, as well.

Bless them.

I'd wanted to ask her how many times Dad cheated on her, but I realized I didn't want to know. But she couldn't have made clearer that she was one of those people who'd *worked it out*.

Good for her. She could work that shit out all she wanted.

Me? Not so much.

Two days later I quit my job at the kindergarten, loaded up my car, and started working my way West.

After, of course, having given my parents explicit instructions to not share my whereabouts with

Vaughn. Which I now know they had no intention of honoring.

That's how the creep ended up in my bathtub.

"Hey, Marn, there's something else I wanted to talk to you about."

Concern crossed her face. "What? Is Tableau not working out? Because I can't give you a job here."

Oh my god. Really?

"Tableau is working out great."

I wasn't sure yet whether to tell her I'd kissed Robbie. Or Maze. So I decided against it.

I took a deep breath. "I wanted to talk to you about taking the yoga teacher training. I'm very interested."

Her eyebrows rose. "Oh. Why didn't it occur to me to suggest that? It sounds perfect for you."

Cool.

"If I do, I will need to stay with you longer," I said slowly, feeling her out. "But hey, I can start paying rent. I... have money now."

I didn't share with her I had three thousand dollars from Robbie hidden in my room. I also didn't tell her my car was repaired. I knew she'd never kick me out, but I just didn't want anyone to know I could leave Denver whenever I wanted to now.

She waved her hand like *don't be silly*. "You can take the class for free," she said, smiling.

I raised my hands in protest. "No, no, no. I can pay. I want to pay."

She shrugged. "You don't have to. But if it makes you feel better..."

Oh my god. I wanted to kiss her. Even if she'd set me up to work with her brother, and had let my deceitful ex-fiancé in our apartment.

"Well, look who it is," a voice resonated from behind me. "The two most beautiful women in Denver."

I whipped around and blushed.

"Hey, Rob," Marni said, reaching for a ringing phone.

I looked at him, the sensation of our kiss the night before replaying itself all the way from my core to the ends of my fingertips.

"You just get here?" he asked, putting his glasses away and scraping his hair back into a ponytail.

Dammit, he smelled good, just like he had last night.

"Um, yeah. Just got here," I stumbled. "Where's baby Jax?"

He took a deep breath. "With his mother. But after last's night's stunt, I now know I could expect the little bugger at any time. Hey, thank you again for your help. You were a total savior."

He took a step closer to me, his gaze solid.

And being the idiot I am, I took a step back. "I'm happy to help anytime. He's a great little guy. So easy going," I chirped.

Robbie nodded, taking my elbow and walking me

away from the front desk. "I also want to thank you for that delicious kiss."

Oh no. He was just putting that shit out there like it was the most normal thing in the world.

Which it might have been for some people. Not me.

"Um, yeah, it was *super*," I stammered. "Well, I have to go change," I said, pointing toward the women's locker room and making a dash for it.

As I pushed the door open, I made the mistake of glancing back over my shoulder.

He was standing there, smiling, and shaking his head.

21

Stell

"HEY, STELL. HOW ARE THINGS GOING?"

Already back at work, I stopped cutting lemons to face Cab, my dimpled former flame. How did the guy I'd secretly lusted after all my life—okay, I'll be honest, had been pretty much in love with all my life—turn out to be such a disappointing douche?

I'd asked myself that for years, until it finally faded from my thoughts.

And now it was back.

Hello!

"Oh. Hi Cab," I said, turning back to my lemons to avoid his gaze.

Four years of college and I was slicing lemons. But

menial as it was, I focused on the bright side. Once I got into a groove, it was kind of like meditating. And I loved getting every last seed out. I looked at it as a personal challenge.

Next, I turned to polishing glasses, another never-ending chore. My spotless glasses were works of art, and I organized them for easy access for when the club was really rolling. The shorter time someone waited for a drink, the sooner they could order another one.

No one had told me that. I'd figured it out for myself.

"You're getting some pretty big guns there from all the lifting you're doing," Cab said, mimicking hand weights.

Why was he so desperate to start a conversation? I continued to ignore him.

But he didn't take the hint.

Big sigh. "You know, Stell, if we have to work together, we're going to need to talk."

Oh, for Christ's sake.

I turned to him, slamming a glass on the bar and flicking my braid back over my shoulder. "Cab, what the hell do you want to talk about? Because in case you haven't noticed, I have a lot to do. It's going to be busy tonight, and I need to get things set up for Maze."

Who hopefully would not find any more evidence of my having crashed the party where he'd kissed me.

Shaking his head, Cab pressed his lips together and looked down.

Yeah. Now he was getting it. *Douche.*

And it wasn't his day to work, so what the hell was he doing here, anyway?

"Stell. Please?"

Against my better judgment, I met his gaze. Which was a mistake. A big, damn mistake. The same sensation I'd gotten from locking eyes with him, ever since I was a prepubescent teenager following him around like the love struck punk that I was, bowled over me like no time had passed, no hearts had been broken, and no one had moved on with their lives.

How did he do that?

After disappearing on me just when I thought he was mine and I was his, the jerk still had the power to jumble my thoughts and make it hard to breathe.

Fuck all. I had enough going on in my life, the latest problem of which was getting rid of my cheating ex-fiancé, without having to deal with anything superfluous like my first love.

There. I'd said it. He was my first love. He knew it, and he took advantage of it.

And he would again.

"Stell, Marni told me what happened with your wedding. I just wanted to say how sorry I am—"

I held a hand up. "Thanks, Cab. It's all for the better. Now can I just—"

He reached for my hand. Dammit. He was touching me now. I wanted to recoil and pretend to be disgusted. But something wouldn't let me.

His two hands held mine gently, as if saying I could pull back if I wanted, but that he hoped I wouldn't.

And those eyes. They showed sorrow. Maybe our parting had been a burden on his heart, too. I'd always assumed he'd just left town and forgotten my ass.

There was more to the story, I was learning.

And while these thoughts were screaming through my mind, tormenting me without mercy, something across the room caught my eye.

What the hell was that?

I craned my neck to see beyond Cab, but the club was dimly lit. I couldn't see the other side of the room clearly.

But I could have sworn Vaughn had been standing there, watching me.

I squinted to see better. There was nothing there now.

"Stell? Are you okay?" Cab asked, looking over his shoulder.

I shook my head, as if that would improve my vision. "Yeah. I thought I saw something strange. But it was just my eyes playing tricks on me."

He squeezed my hand as if to offer support and dammit, my cold heart melted a little.

Just a little.

But I pulled my hand out of his anyway. There had been enough touching for one day.

"Stell, how are you enjoying Denver?"

I was going to get sucked into his small talk, despite trying to avoid it.

I shrugged. "It's fine. You know, a nice place for a short stay. But I will eventually hit the road for LA. It's just a matter of time."

He smiled at me, and my heart thumped in my chest. "You're doing a great job for us. We all really appreciate it. Things have never run so smoothly."

I looked over his shoulder again. Had I really seen Vaughn? Or was it someone who looked like him? I wouldn't put it past him to show up at Tableau, under some stupid pretense, just so he could keep an eye on me.

Jesus. What would get rid of that creep once and for all?

And like it always had, Cab's smile smacked me right in the gut. I was quickly losing my resolve to remain mean. And bitter.

I continued babbling. "I'm enjoying Tableau. It's not a forever thing, but it's been a great opportunity to get back on track. I guess you know that on my way into town, Robbie plowed into my car."

He nodded, trying to look serious. Then, he broke out in a smile again. "I'm sorry. It's just kind of funny. That you ended up working with him."

I guess I could see the irony in it, now that I'd been paid, and I was pretty much over having almost been ripped off. And I *had* kissed Robbie in the upstairs office, after all.

So that feud was over.

"I can offer you a tip that might make your job easier," he said, leaning closer.

"Really? What's that?" Aside from the manual labor, which I'd pretty much gotten used to, the job really wasn't that hard.

But I'd hear him out.

"Even though you're not pouring drinks, at least not yet, it's helpful to know what's in each cocktail. That way you can anticipate the bar's needs better. Don't tell anybody, but when I was learning all the drinks, I made myself flash cards."

Good old flash cards. Like learning math.

"Why can't I tell anyone? What's the big deal?"

He looked around, like anybody cared about his big secret. "Because. It's super nerdy."

I snickered. I couldn't help it.

He wrinkled his brow, clearly stricken by my laughing.

"Sorry, Cab, but you're right. That is super nerdy."

He gradually smiled, the dimples popping up again as if to say *look how fucking cute I am.*

I hated that about him. Actually, I hated a few things about Cab. But I might be willing to work on them.

"Hey, look. It's a company meeting."

We turned to find Robbie and Maze making their way behind the bar toward us.

Oh my god oh my god.

The three of these guys right here, all together, looking at none other than *me*.

I gripped the bar to hide my shaking hands.

I'd kissed two of them, and the third, well, I didn't want to think about the past.

Maze raised his hand to high-five me. "Stell, we're gonna tear it up tonight, right?" he asked with a big smile.

"Um, yeah," I said, returning his high five and looking desperately for something to wipe, clean, or polish.

But I was pretty much caught up on my work. Dammit.

So I started wiping the bar anyway. Could never be too clean.

I looked down at the wood as if I could rub out some ancient sort of scratch and hide the heated blush that started at my neck, ran to my forehead, and was now causing sweaty drops on my temples.

"Hey, Stell, careful over there. You'll wear out the bar," Robbie said.

I looked up and damn if all three weren't staring right at me with huge smiles.

Shit, shit, shit.

I took a deep breath. "Would you guys excuse me? I'm going to run to the ladies' room before we get busy."

"Do your thing, darlin'," Robbie sang.

Was he kidding? Calling me darlin'?

I don't think so.

I darted into the far bathroom stall and sat with my head in my hands while I composed myself. Or *tried* to compose myself. How in the hell was I supposed to work with three of the most beautiful men I'd ever seen in my life when every time they got close to me I started to shake and sweat?

All of whom I'd kissed.

But I wouldn't be working with them forever. I needed to keep that in mind.

I'd do my yoga teacher training and get to LA, hopefully sometime soon. Palm trees and beaches were just around the corner for me.

I forced myself to exit the bathroom stall and looked in the mirror to fix my lip gloss and hair.

Not that I cared how I looked. I mean, I cared. But it wasn't for the guys.

Not at all.

Taking a deep breath, I yanked open the ladies' room door to get back to work.

And as I did, I ran smack into Cab.

"Oh. Excuse me," I said, trying to sidestep him.

But he sidestepped at the same time.

"Oops, sorry," I said, trying again.

That's when it occurred to me that I was cornered, and it wasn't by accident.

I mean, I could certainly get away. Really. If I wanted to.

"Cab. You're in my way."

I hated to state the obvious, but I had to say something.

He held his hands up. "Wait. Stell. I just wanted a moment with you."

I put my hands on my hips. "What? What do you want?" I demanded, hoping my shaking wasn't obvious.

He took a step closer. "It's just… it's just so good to see you after all this time. You have no idea how much I—"

I didn't want to hear any more. I ducked around him and ran down the stairs toward the bar.

Smartest thing I'd done all day.

22

Cab

WELL, shit.

I'd thought I'd be immune to Stell. So much time had gone by. I was sure she wouldn't mean a thing to me like she once had.

But the moment I touched her hand and moved closer, close enough to remember the gold flecks in her eyes and the little scar on her forehead from a long-ago bike wreck, all that had been alive in me way back when exploded. Like it had been waiting under the surface for an opportunity to tell me I'd fucked up the best thing in my life.

It wasn't like I hadn't known what I lost when I let my dad pressure me into leaving Philly. At first, I'd thought it would be easy to walk away. When I finally got my head out of my ass and realized I'd made a terrible mistake, it was too late to rectify the situation.

Plain and simple, my father did not want me to be with Estella Kline. He hated her congressman father and his politics, and I suspected had even more grievances against him that I was not aware of. That's all there was to it. I let my father insert a wedge between us in a way that only a terrible, selfish man like he could conceive of, and an immature and intimidated kid like I was at the time, would allow.

There would be no going back. It was too late. Too much time had passed, and her heart was too full of hate for me.

I couldn't blame her. Not one bit.

But I didn't know how to let it go, especially now that she was more beautiful than ever, a mature version of the young girl whose virginity I'd taken.

And then disappeared the next day.

I'd had my eye on her half my life. Starting with the moment she began palling around with my little sister, I was barely able to take my eyes off her, even when I was a punky jerk who wouldn't have given one of my sister's friends the time of day. It was a secret I held close from everyone.

Well, almost everyone.

Marni knew. She always knew.

My sister had uncanny powers of observation, even when she was just a kid. She comprehended the things she saw with a maturity well beyond her years. And even now, if I didn't know better, I'd swear from time to time she could read minds.

And being the awesome sister she was, even when we were fighting like cats and dogs, she never breathed a word of my infatuation with Stell to a single soul.

Although she'd admitted to *me* what she knew. But she never told anyone else.

I'd always suspected she'd also observed Stell's interest in me. I may have pretended to see nothing, but I wasn't blind. And again, out of the same loyalty to her friend that she also had for me, she said nothing.

Those years of pretending to ignore each other turned into longing glances, and still neither of us acted on our feelings. Partly because we didn't know how to, and partly because it would have been so predictable.

Not that we knew that then.

We'd known each other so long that the familiarity between us was almost painful.

When we'd finally spent time together, just the two of us, we danced around our attraction until the night we fell into bed together—out in my parents' pool house—and my father caught us. He hadn't walked in on us or anything like that, but the next day he could see it all over my face. He nipped things in the bud real fast by putting me on the next plane out of town.

I'd been warned to never contact her again.

He'd told me she wasn't a nice girl and came from

an even worse family. That all these years he'd just tolerated the Klines because the girls were such good friends, and that he despised the congressman going back to some dispute my father had been on the losing end of so long ago no one remembered exactly what it had been over.

His interference was horrible, but my acceptance of it was even worse. I'd never forgive myself. I didn't know how to make it right. Or if it were even possible to do so.

This was the same father who wanted to pull the plug on Tableau in order to force me back to Philly to take over the reins of his hedge fund business.

Something I had no aptitude for, and no interest in.

But he didn't care about that.

He wanted to keep the family money in the family, and the only way to pull that off was with a succession plan that included me.

No matter what the cost.

23

Cab

"Dude. You look like you just lost your best friend," Robbie said, smacking me on the back the next day.

I looked between him and Maze, who'd just arrived for our weekly meeting. We were in a booth in one of our private rooms where we could speak undisturbed and uninterrupted. The support staff that buzzed around cleaning and preparing knew that this was our time and that the only reason to interfere was if the building was on fire.

I rolled my head around in an attempt to stretch some of the tension out of my neck. I'd had a damn headache for hours that no amount of aspirin would chase away, and it was making me seriously pissy.

"I'm fucked guys. Just totally fucked," I said.

Maze tried not to laugh, because he could be a dick that way, but Robbie's face was crossed with concern.

It was a good thing that he was a father and not Maze.

"Okay, Cab. Tell us what the hell is going on. It is your dad again?" Robbie asked.

Dad. I still had to deal with his bullshit. But at that moment in time, my main concern was Stell. And the guys needed to know.

"I... I'm not sure you guys are aware, but Stell and I have some history between us."

Maze slammed his hand on the table between us and looked at Robbie. "I *told* you, didn't I? I knew there was something going on."

Robbie nodded slowly. "Yup. You told me, Maze."

I buried my head in my hands. "Is it that obvious?"

"Actually, no, it's not that obvious, Cab. It's just that I know you, and when I saw you watching Stell, and knowing that you all pretty much grew up together, it wasn't hard to figure out there was a story there."

"She lost her virginity to me."

The room was silent for a moment before Robbie let out a long, low whistle.

"Damn," Maze said. "That's some serious shit."

"It didn't end well. And I'm not proud of it. But guys, I look at her now, years later, and she's sassier and more beautiful than ever. I can't deny the attraction."

Maze and Robbie looked at each other again.

"What?" I asked. "What's going on? Did one of you guys already ask her out?"

Robbie rubbed his hands together like he did when he was thinking. "Like you, we're interested in her, too."

Oh. Wow. This could be a good thing.

Weird but good.

"No kidding."

"Yeah," Maze said, nodding.

"Think she'll go for it?" I asked.

More silence.

And I understood why.

We guys had a thing for dating the same woman. And it usually worked out well. That was, however, when we had a woman who was interested in our sort of alternative arrangement.

Just the year before, we'd all three dated a beautiful girl from Paris named Esme. Her student visa had eventually run out and she'd had to return, but the time we'd had with her was magical. I'd always thought Maze would follow her to France, but he'd decided against it. He was a solitary guy, and a traditional sort of relationship, with one guy and one girl, wasn't his cup of tea.

However, our *sharing* one woman certainly was.

And now it looked like all three of us were interested in the lovely Stell.

Damn.

"I… would doubt she's ever even considered a relationship along the lines of what we like. But I think we should feel her out. If she seems responsive to each of us, then we can propose it to her."

Maze threw his hands in the air. "Well, I've already kissed her."

My head snapped in his direction. "Seriously? When?"

"At the private party we had a week ago. She was in costume. I didn't know it was her until the next day when she had some tinsel from the wig stuck in her hair. I haven't told her I know."

Robbie burst out laughing. "Well shit. I've kissed her too."

Jesus. Was I the only one late to the party?

"When did you kiss her, Robbie?" I asked.

"The other night. When Elise dropped off Jax with no heads up, Stell took him up to the office to babysit. I was so turned on by how freaking awesome she was with him I couldn't help myself."

Well, shit.

"She is fucking awesome, guys. I never would have left her except my dad more or less forced me," I admitted.

Saying it out loud made me sick to my stomach. What I'd done was wrong and it disgusted me.

"How did he do that?" Robbie asked. "And why?"

"He hates her dad, Congressman Kline. They have some long-standing feud. And he convinced me it would never work between us. I was young and listened to him, like the fool that I was. He shipped me to Denver and here I am today."

I couldn't believe I'd never shared this story with the guys. We all knew each other's dirt. Well, most of it, anyway.

And I knew all too well why I'd not shared it. Plain and simple, I was ashamed.

I was still ashamed, in fact.

"I'm working with her tonight," I said. "I'll feel her out, but I have a feeling she pretty much still hates me and probably always will."

But I sure as hell hoped not.

"STELL, you've been watching the girls dancing on the platforms all night."

She looked away, embarrassed. "Well, it looks kind of fun. Like they get up there, they're suddenly someone else. They just dance their hearts out."

We watched one of our floor staff usher a girl off a platform and then a new one onto it. It was pretty tightly controlled for safety reasons. We didn't need anyone getting hurt.

"You want to try it, don't you?" I asked.

She wrinkled her nose. "No. No way. Of course not."

Mmmm hmmm.

"C'mon. Give it a shot," I said, pushing her toward the end of the bar.

She shook her head hard. "No. I don't think so. It wouldn't be a good idea. Plus, I'm working."

I put my hands on her shoulders, and damn did it feel good to touch her. "Go. I know you like to dance. I remember that about you."

She took a couple steps toward the end of the bar and turned around to look at me.

"Go for it. You'll regret it if you don't," I insisted.

A smile broke out across her face and she pulled her shoulders back. With a deep breath, she scooted out the end of the bar and skipped up the stairs to the second floor, where the dance platforms were accessed.

I finished making one of those dreadful muddled cocktails and when I looked up, saw Stell step gingerly onto the platform. It was about twelve feet above the dance floor with a railing around it. Spotlights shone all around, flashing in time to whatever house music was blaring.

She walked further onto the platform, and looked out over the floor. Then she looked over at me.

I pumped my hand in the air. "Do it," I bellowed.

That got the attention of everyone at the bar, and most of the people on the dance floor. They all turned toward Stell and starting chanting, "Do it, do it."

For a second she was horrified, and I was afraid she was going to run back off the platform before even giving it a shot. But she didn't.

She lifted her arms above her head and, closing her eyes, began to sway to the music, responding exactly how I'd hoped she would. In seconds, she'd lost herself, and everyone watching began cheering her on.

And I'd be lying if I didn't admit that her tight jeans, and the way she swung her hair around her head, were giving me the beginning of an erection that was making my pants awfully uncomfortable.

Just then, I heard a loud crash, and a fight broke out on the dance floor, something that happened from time to time. I immediately looked up at Stell, whose eyes had opened wide in fear. She turned and started to run off the platform. I shouted for her to stay where she was, but she didn't hear me.

The bouncers arrived in seconds and jumped into the brawl. From my spot behind the bar, I couldn't see much of what was going on, but I was able to track Stell running down the stairs in an attempt to get back behind the bar. I waved my arms for her to stay away from the ruckus, but in her panic she got too close to it. A guy who'd just been sucker punched went flying onto his back and Stell was just close enough to be taken down by him.

She was thrown to the floor and he fell on top of her. The guy scrambled to his feet.

But Stell didn't.

24

Stell

"Here. Try a little water."

I looked up to find Cab cradling me in his arms, holding a bottle of water to my lips. I took a couple sips and touched a wet spot on my temple.

When I withdrew my fingers, I saw they were spotted with blood.

"How did I get up here?" I asked, looking around the private room where I was sprawled on one of the booth benches.

"I carried you up here. You scared me. You were knocked out in the fight that broke out on the dance floor."

I tried to push myself up and realized a vicious

headache was circling my head. "I think I'd better take an aspirin. Can you help me sit up?"

Cab put his hands under my arms and gently pushed me off his lap, but continued holding on to me.

My head spun for a moment and then cleared. "Whew."

He propped me into a corner of the booth where I could lean while my head cleared. "Rest here. I'll go get some aspirin."

I watched him run out of the room and a little twinge in my heart reminded me how I'd once felt about him.

Holy shit. How did I go from dancing like a go-go girl to being knocked onto my ass in some sort of barroom brawl?

Not what I'd been expecting to happen at work today.

Cab returned, handing me two aspirin.

"Who's working the bar?" I asked, sipping my water.

He took a seat next to me. *Right* next to me. In fact, he put an arm around me and pulled me to him.

Holy crap.

It was all a bit more familiar than I was comfortable with, but under the circumstances I figured I'd go with it. I tilted my head just enough to peer up. The closeness felt good. I couldn't lie.

Damn him.

"Maze is down there. We're closing soon anyway because of the fight."

"What caused it?"

He scraped his fingers through his dirty blond hair, pulling it back and off his worried forehead. "I don't know for sure, but we think someone's coming into the club and selling drugs."

Oh my god. I was working in a place where drugs were being sold?

I bolted to my feet, entirely too fast. "I'm not sure I like the sound of that at all." I gripped the table to hide my residual wooziness. So much for sounding badass and intolerant of thugs.

"Slow down," Cab said, grabbing my hand.

We looked at his hand holding mine and then we looked back at each other.

I couldn't do this. I wouldn't do this. I started to pull away, but he held my hand tighter.

"Will you sit back down?" he asked, pulling gently. "Just for a few minutes?"

I didn't like the look in his eyes. It was contrite. Too contrite. And the problem with that was if he asked for forgiveness for what he'd done, I'm not sure I could tell him to go fuck himself.

The tough girl in me, such as it was, had fantasized so many times about this moment, where I could give him a piece of my mind, and hurt him back just the way he'd hurt me. I'd deliver a litany of words, which ones I wasn't even sure, that would take him down a notch and that he'd never forget. He'd realize what a mistake he'd made, and regret it for the rest of his life.

My words would be a metaphorical knife right to his heart. Because that's what he deserved.

Disappearing on me, the very day after he'd popped my cherry.

Yeah, I don't think so, buddy. You don't get away with shit like that and live to tell about it.

In fact, the more I thought about it, the more I was getting pissed.

But I sat back down anyway. Damn him and his light blue eyes. I was weak. And I hated myself for it.

Besides, I didn't have much choice with the way he was holding my damn hand. I could have yanked it out of his grip, kicked him in the shin, and run, but as much fun as it was to imagine that, I knew I wouldn't. His hand felt good on mine. Warm. Safe. Caring.

Jesus, I needed to have my head examined.

"You know, Cab, this kind of reminds me of how we ended up together last time, back in your parents' pool house."

He pressed his lips together and something I was pretty sure was regret washed over his face.

Good.

"Stell, I want to say I'm sorry," he started, but his voice cracked.

Oh, brother. I was a sucker for a sensitive guy, but I wasn't falling for this bullshit.

"Words are so insufficient to make up for what I did." He looked down and shook his head.

Well, damn. I can't say that didn't pull on my heart-strings a bit.

I wanted to let him make me feel better. But I also wanted to tell him to go to hell. These conflicting feelings whiplashed through my head without mercy, pulling me in opposite directions, rather than offering comfort.

I didn't want to hear his excuses. And yet I did. The contradictions swirling around both amused and disgusted me.

Were they signs of weakness or strength?

Did it really matter?

"Not a day has gone by that I haven't thought about you," he said.

Oh Christ. He was wearing me down.

He put a finger under my chin and turned my face to him. I obviously knew what was coming—I wasn't an idiot—but my heart raced nonetheless, and I wondered if he'd like kissing me like he had years before.

Only one way to find out.

25

Stell

I LEANED my face toward his and closed my eyes, holding my breath for our first contact. And when our lips met, it was like nothing bad had ever happened between us. He was firm and demanding like he'd always been, devouring me until all thoughts of resistance disappeared. I was flying, yet moored by his strong hands, which wove through my hair to pull me closer.

"You are so beautiful. I've missed you," he breathed. "I hope you can someday forgive me. Until you do, I can't forgive myself."

I looked away, needing to avoid his gaze to organize my thoughts. "It… was rough, Cab. I'm not gonna lie."

An hour before, I never would have admitted that to him out of fear of giving him some sort of sick satisfaction. But now I realized he was anything *but* satisfied with the choices he'd made.

He was living with years of regret.

I'd been hurt, but I'd done nothing wrong. In time, my heart had healed. Mostly.

It was a different story for him.

And then I realized, I could have compassion for him, *and* for myself. Forgiving him wasn't letting him get away with it, and there was no need for me to punish him endlessly. He'd been punishing himself.

I squeezed his hand. I couldn't say it. I wasn't ready. But I would be some day.

"I have something else to tell you," he said.

What else was there?

"The other guys like you, too."

Huh? What the hell did that mean? Of course, I'd kissed them both, but those were just flukes, right?

Right?

He pulled back, smoothing my hair and examining every inch of my face like he'd never seen it before. "We guys do this… thing. We *share*."

Um, okay.

He nodded at my obvious confusion. "I know it's unconventional, but we all like to date the same woman, when we find the right one. I mean, we have to all be interested in her, and then of course, she has to be into it too."

Cripes, I'd thought I was dizzy before. Good thing I was sitting.

"So, you guys have like a ménage sort of thing, except it's all three of you?"

He thought for a moment. "Well, yeah. It's like that. Look, obviously you and I have history together, but I know Robbie likes you, and so does Maze."

Shit. Did he know I'd kissed them both?

"You've kissed both of them, and that's totally cool. In fact, I find it hot as shit."

I side-eyed him because I didn't know what else to do. "How do you know that?"

He shrugged. "They told me."

Big mouths.

But wait. How did Maze know he'd kissed me?

"I was wearing a costume the night I kissed Maze—"

"He knew it was you. I think he figured it out later."

Damn. I'd thought I was so clever. So much for Marni's brilliant costumes.

"What are you doing?" a shrill voice called from the doorway.

I reflexively moved several inches away from Cab, before I even saw that it was psycho Annabel acting like she was the morality police.

Really, lady?

"Why do you care?" I snapped back.

I was tired of her shit.

"I'll have you know that I am telling everyone I caught you two together—"

"Annabel, shut up. Just shut up. And after you shut up, please go to hell," Cab said, turning back to me to kiss me even more passionately than before.

She gaped at our insolence in the face of her scolding, and stomped off.

As soon as she was gone, I looked at Cab. "That was seriously funny. I mean, who's she going to tell? The school principal?"

I started laughing. Like *I couldn't stop* kind of laughing.

And because laughter was contagious, Cab joined me, shaking, and doubling over at the absurdity of her threat.

And maybe also the absurdity of life.

"Why'd you do it?" I finally asked.

I'd waited so long for an answer to this, I wasn't even sure I really wanted it.

What if he said it was because I sucked in bed?

Or that he never really cared about me anyway?

It was best not to ask the questions you didn't really want answers to.

He took a deep breath. "I'm not proud of this, but I let my dad pressure me into it. As soon as he found out about us, he put me on the next plane to Denver."

Holy shit. Mr. Hendricks had been behind it. I'd always wondered.

"And he's not done messing with my life," Cab

continued, running a finger down my cheek and over my bottom lip.

God, the effect he had on me.

"What's he doing to you now?" I asked, in between licking and sucking his finger.

Cab's eyelids got heavy and he shifted, no doubt making room for an erection.

"He wants me to come back and work in the family business. And to force my hand, he's demanding back the investment he made in Tableau. Or, threatening to sell us."

I'd always thought that man was horrible, and not just because my parents couldn't stand him. It was a miracle Cab and Marni turned out as well as they did.

"God. I had no idea. What will you do?"

"The guys and I are hoping that by having private parties like we did last week, we might raise enough money to quickly to pay him back and get him out of our hair. He's such an asshole he doesn't even care that his pulling the plug on Tableau would put a shit load of people out of work, not to mention my business partners, Maze and Robbie."

"What can I do to help?" I asked.

He laughed. "Unless you have a spare quarter of a million dollars lying around, not much. But thank you for asking," he said, kissing me on the forehead.

"Hey, I think we'd better get downstairs to see if Maze needs any help."

Cab glanced at his watch. His very expensive watch.

I remembered when Mr. Hendricks gave one to both Cab and Marni. He'd said they would be family heirlooms. He was into shit like that.

Pretentious, was what my father called it.

But I never told Cab or Marni that.

"So your dad didn't want you involved with me, huh?"

While I wasn't surprised, saying the words out loud was a little like pouring salt on a wound.

Cab opened his mouth, closing it just as fast.

I got it. He didn't need to say it.

I'd been through enough that I could face the truth. If the man didn't want me with his son, that said more about him than it did me.

Not my fucking problem.

But Cab was compelled to explain, anyway. "You're right, Stell. He didn't want us together. It has nothing to do with you, though. It's between our parents, involving some long-standing insult someone visited on the other, that the old fuckers just can't get past," he said.

Thank god for distance and the passage of time. It seemed like a lifetime ago that any of that had happened.

Now, I had a completely new set of challenges to conquer. And, as if they weren't enough, Cab had just piled a new one on me with his *sharing* proposal.

I couldn't say I understood what the hell he was

talking about, but I had to be honest. I was massively attracted to all three of the Tableau bartenders.

But that didn't mean I could date all three of them.

And besides, I was leaving for LA.

Right?

26

Maze

"LET HIM GO, GUYS."

Two of the biggest bouncers we'd ever had at Tableau released the drug dealer with enough of a push to send him stumbling over his own feet.

"Fuck you guys," Grant spat at them, straightening himself out. "And fuck you too, Maze."

I shook my head. "You can't sell drugs here, Grant. I've told you that."

He rolled his eyes. "I don't know what you're talking about."

He was not only a lousy drug dealer, but he was also a lousy liar.

I nodded at one of the bouncers, who produced a handful of little bags of white powder.

"These were in your pocket. I suppose they just walked there by themselves?"

Avoiding my gaze, Grant stared at the packets, most likely contemplating what he'd have to do to get them back.

I *knew* that fucker was selling drugs in my club.

"I've known you a long time, Grant. I considered you a friend. But your activities here are over. You're not welcome in the club anymore."

He clenched his fists. I knew he wouldn't go away easily.

"C'mon, Maze. Tableau's the hottest club in town. You can't lock me out."

I took the packets of coke from the bouncer and held them up to Grant. "Sorry, man. I've given you enough warnings. Next time you have a spat with someone, bullets could start flying for all we know. For fuck's sake, dude, one of my employees got hurt tonight."

More than anything, that's what pissed me off. I'd missed it, being up in the office, but the panic on Cab's face when he'd brought Stell up to the private party room told me all I needed to know to make a decision. I blasted downstairs to take care of the problem.

"I bring so many people here, Maze. You know that," Grant said.

I had a feeling Tableau would survive just fine without his posse of cokeheads.

"Grant. If you want this coke back, you have to agree to stay away. You will never return to the club."

I had a feeling I knew which would hurt him more—losing the coke I was holding in my hand over having to find a new place to sell it.

He held his hand out, as I knew he would. He could find another place to deal. The drugs in my hands were worth at least a thousand bucks, I estimated. He'd want them back at any price.

"You're agreeing with me? That you won't come back here?" I asked.

"Fuck you, man. Yes, I agree. Now give me my stuff."

Asshole. He could cost us everything we had. I was not going to let that happen.

I threw the packets at his feet so he could scramble for them.

"Good. Get your shit and get the fuck out," I said.

Now on his knees, Grant grabbed his drugs and stuffed them into his pockets. When he was done, he rose, looked at me and the bouncers as if to assess whether he could have the last word, and stormed toward the door, turning around one more time to flip us off.

"Ooooh, tough guy," Cab said from behind me, laughing at Grant's last minute attempt to save face.

I turned to the bouncers. "Good job tonight, guys. I appreciate it."

They nodded and hit the road. They'd had a long night.

There was noise on the steps from the mezzanine, and I turned to see Cab slowly walking Stell down the steps.

"Well, here she is. My hard working, beleaguered barback," I said, pulling her to me.

It might have been overly familiar, hugging her, but she'd been knocked out on the job and I wanted her to know she was safe now.

And I was happy to report she embraced me right back, burrowing her face against my chest.

I took her by the arms to look her over. "You're feeling better?"

The club's front door blew open and Robbie rushed in. "I got here as fast as I could. Is everything under control?" he asked, rushing straight for Stell.

She had a little laugh and put her hands up. "I'm fine, guys. I really am. Cab took good care of me."

Yeah, I bet that bastard did.

"Thank you," she said, looking at all of us. "I really appreciate the concern. And fast action."

She gestured in Cab's direction, and I could swear I saw embarrassment wash over his face. I knew he had a thing for her, but damn.

"Hey, Rob, would you lock the front door?" I asked, pointing.

"Yeah, man. Everybody else gone?"

"Yup."

Stell walked behind the bar and began to look around. "Jesus. I'm gone for an hour, and everything here goes to shit," she laughed, starting to put dirty glasses in the dishwasher.

"Stell, stop working. Just chill."

We settled in at the bar. I loved the club after hours. Sometimes it was eerie, having gone from a pulsing creature full of life to complete stillness, but I looked at it as giving our baby a little rest.

Crazy.

"Stell, why don't you open one of those bottles of champagne in the back of the cooler? I've been saving them for a special occasion," Cab said.

She tilted her head, and damn if her eyes didn't bewitch all three of us at once. "This is a special occasion? What's so special about it?" She smiled, hands on hips.

All right. She was being saucy. I liked that.

Cab gestured toward the cooler. "Get the champagne, will ya? For Christ's sake, you're alive. Isn't that reason to celebrate?"

She delivered four champagne flutes and then started moving bottles to get at the stuff we hid in the far recesses of one of our fridges.

When she put a bottle on the bar, I reached for it. "Here. Let me do it."

She shimmied her shoulders. "Such a gentleman."

Fuck. She was flirting. That was a good sign.

I popped the champagne cork and poured.

Cab held up his glass. "To the past, and to the future," he said, his gaze not moving from Stell.

"Cheers," everyone said.

Robbie set his glass down. "Now, Stell, I hear your new career in go-go dancing is what got you knocked out tonight."

She hung her head and when she looked back up, she was blushing. "Exactly. That's what I get for being a hussy," she laughed.

Robbie gestured toward the platform, now looming above the empty dance floor. "I say give it another shot. You were interrupted earlier by an inconsiderate drug dealer who started a fight. It's only fair you get another chance."

She broke into a huge smile and turned a shoulder toward us, playing shy.

Only we knew better.

"It's so nerve-wracking up there," she giggled.

"Only one way to get over that, sweetie," Cab added.

"Well, I guess I could. Just once. Especially for Denver's Most Eligible Bachelor."

Maze groaned while Stell took a swig of her champagne and headed for the mezzanine.

27

Maze

THE DJ HAD long since gone home, but we had access to the speaker system from the bar. I scrolled through my Pandora stations and turned on Pony by Ginuwine. It was an oldie, but it was one of my favorites and I thought it might get Stell fired up.

"Woo, look at Stell," Robbie hollered through megaphone hands.

She leaned on the platform railing and slowly began to move her hips back and forth, her gaze locked on us. Kicking off her sneakers, she tossed them to us and began to slide her sock-covered feet over the platform.

And holy fuck if she wasn't sexy. With her hands

above her head and hair whipping around her face, she twisted and twirled, shaking her ass until my dick ached with a raging hard on.

I lowered the volume on the music a couple notches. "C'mon Stell! Take it off!"

Her eyes popped open and she looked as if to assess how serious I was.

I nodded at her, and she winked back.

That's what I'm talking about.

Continuing to grind, she grabbed hold of the bottom of her T-shirt and played with the hem, inching it up to show her flat stomach and then pulling it back down in pretend modesty. Turning her back to us in a tease, she continued pulling the shirt up and down until she finally pulled it over her head and chucked it to the floor below. She peeked at us from over her shoulder and crossed her arms over her chest.

Damn, she was good at this.

Then, she turned to face us, still gyrating to the music, hands over her bra-covered breasts. She kneaded them, her head dropping back in ecstasy.

"Fuck, man," Robbie said, his eyes wide. "I didn't know she had that in her."

I guess when you get knocked flat on your ass by some brawling guys you could either shrink like a victim, or tell the rest of the world to kiss your ass. Like she was right now.

The song played on while Stell opened her jeans

and slowly—very slowly—pushed them down her hips. I was dying to see her beautiful ass, and when she finally turned around in her lacy thong and showed us the goods, I nearly creamed my jeans.

Holy shit.

With her back to us, she bent all the way forward as she pulled her socks and jeans over her feet, giving us a perfect view of her lace-covered pussy.

Fuck, I was tempted to excuse myself for the men's room, but I didn't want to miss a moment of her performance. I readjusted myself in my constraining blue jeans and looked at Cab and Robbie, who were basically doing the same thing.

Stell, now clothed only in her thong and matching bra, tossed her jeans from the railing.

God, I was dying to run my hands over that beautiful, smooth skin.

When the music wound down, she danced her way back to us at the bar. It was like she couldn't stop.

Which worked just fine for me.

"Guys. Think our girl would like to visit the Playroom for a bit?" I suggested.

Cab slammed his hand on the bar. "I fucking hope so."

He got off his barstool and approached her, speaking in her ear. She smiled back up him and took his hand. I grabbed another bottle of champagne, Robbie got the glasses, and we headed up.

WHEN WE GOT THERE, Cab was already kissing Stell, so Robbie and I grabbed seats. I was dying to get my hands on her, as I'm sure Robbie was, but watching also got me hot as hell. It was part of sharing. If you didn't like watching, sharing was not for you.

But we three were on the same page. And had been for a while. I remembered for a moment watching Cab and Robbie tag-team our French girl, Esme. The memory had given me countless hours of jerking off pleasure. I imagined it always would. At least until we formed new memories. Like we were just then.

"Fuck this," Robbie said, getting up and joining Cab and Stell.

He embraced her from behind, and she ground her bottom into his crotch like a little tease. He unhooked her bra and moved for her tits, which he began to pull and twist until she moaned into Cab's mouth, which she was still kissing.

Robbie slipped her thong down to her ankles and helped her step out of it. Positioning himself right behind her, her pulled open her ass cheeks and buried his face as deeply as he could, licking her from top to bottom.

That's my Robbie. Ass man all the way.

In response, Stell arched and pushed her bottom further into his face.

I readjusted myself in my pants for about the tenth

time, wondering if I should join in or just let Stell enjoy the two guys, especially since it was her first time with the three of us.

I wondered if she knew I'd figured out who she was the night of the costume party. That had been fucking hilarious, and she'd been so hot with her tinsel-y wig and clingy silver jumpsuit, which, by the way, she'd not worn a bra under.

I'd known right away we'd want to invite her to our kinky little world. And I'd had a pretty good feeling she might accept.

Cab said he'd mentioned our proposal to her earlier. Things were looking like she might just be into it.

The guys laid Stell back on a sofa, with Robbie's face buried in her pussy while Cab licked and sucked her tits. I'd had enough of all the watching, so I walked over to the sofa, where I whipped out my cock and put it in Stell's hand. Her eyes widened with surprise, and a grin spread across her face as she began to stroke me.

Damn, her grip felt nice. I rocked my hips into it, fucking her hand while holding my dick at the root. I wasn't going to last long, that much I knew. It had been too long since I'd been with a woman, and too long that I'd been drooling over Stell.

Robbie pulled his face out from between her legs and I got my first look at her pretty pink pussy. She was neatly trimmed down there like I'd imagined she'd be.

"Look at the lovely girl jerking Maze's dick," he said.

She smiled and as soon as Robbie got back to sucking on her clit, she arched into his mouth and began tossing her head back and forth.

Our baby was going to come.

"Oh fuck," she murmured while Cab still played with her tits and she worked my dick. "Robbie, yeah, I'm gonna come."

"Come in his mouth, darlin', because I'm about to come on you."

I pushed Cab out of the way, and jerked myself all over her tits.

She screamed, bucking and arching and pushing Robbie's head into her pussy. With her free hand, she rubbed my cum into her tits.

Jesus Christ.

That's when Cab pulled out his own stiff cock. "Baby, you're not done yet. I'm gonna give you more."

She watched Cab stroked himself and explode on her chest just like I had.

Robbie, still going to town on her pussy, thrust two fingers inside her and while she rubbed cum into her tits, she arched her back and began to scream.

"Oh my god, yes. Oh. Oh," she cried, spasming into his mouth.

Holy fuck. That was one of the most intense things I'd ever experienced, and I think the guys felt the same as evidenced by their wide-eyed surprise. I whipped my shirt off over my head and began to clean Stell up with it, who laughed and grabbed it from me to finish the job.

"I knew you guys were kinky fuckers," she said as Cab helped her sit up.

I'd been pretty sure she was a kinky fucker, too.

28

Stell

I'D HEARD OF THREESOMES, but never foursomes.

Maybe that was a thing in Denver? Because I was pretty sure it wasn't a thing in Philly. But then, what did I know? I'd been engaged to a douchebag who'd cheated on me with one of my bridesmaids. So, clearly, I was going through life with my head up my ass.

Speaking of asses, I'd not seen or heard from Vaughn for several days and was hoping—no, praying —that he'd given up on me and headed back to Philly. I really didn't get why the hell he'd come after me to begin with. Was he really that dumb?

In order to get some intel, Marni did some snooping with the 'old gang.' Seems that as soon as I left town, Suza, the bridesmaid who'd gotten cozy with Vaughn, had cut him loose. She was only interested in him as long as he was attached to me.

How fucked was that?

Either way, she was my ex-friend now. Marni's too.

Because I was still pretending my car was in the shop, and was tired of spending money on Uber, Marni had offered me her bike. It was only five or six miles to the club, so I started riding every day. At the end of a shift, one of the guys usually piled the bike in the back of their car and gave me a lift home.

It was funny, but things were almost perfect. Simple. Uncomplicated.

Well, uncomplicated except that now I'd been with all three guys. All at once. Not one at a time, like normal people. No, I'd gotten down and dirty in one big, zesty session.

And it had been amazing.

I still don't know what came over me. Maybe it was getting knocked out and realizing I could get right back up without a scratch. It was like I was compelled to give the world the middle finger, and tell it I could be a bad ass, too. The whole thing kicked off some sort of rebellion in me.

Like no one could keep me down.

Although, a few days later I was reconsidering whether I'd made a mistake or not. I mean, as fun as it was, nothing could come of it. I wasn't sure exactly what the guys had in mind suggesting I date the three of them, but I was pretty certain it was something that could only end in disaster and multiple broken hearts, mine included. And while I was enjoying Denver, I wasn't in it for the long haul. LA was still calling, although my obsession with it was tempered. I'd get there eventually.

But I couldn't stop thinking about how natural it felt to be with them. Even Cab. I would have thought it would be awkward as hell to get together with him—the guy I lost my virginity to, and then who disappeared without a word—but I knew what it was like to be manipulated and pressured by parents. I guess I had forgiven him.

Everyone knew his dad was a bastard, so his sending Cab away was just par for the course. And Mr. Hendricks was well aware that taking him from me would hurt my parents, too. He'd succeeded.

"Hey, Maze," I said, coming through the club's front door.

An hour away from opening, the place was completely quiet. I loved it like this.

Looking up from his inventory sheet, he shot me a smile that nearly melted already-wobbly legs. He was just so perfect with his manly, sculpted jaw and broad shoulders.

The stuff women dream of.

And now that I'd messed around with him and found he was about a hundred times more skilled than

Vaughn, I'd realized what a shitty choice I'd made in ever committing to that weasel.

"It's awesome you're riding a bike in. Between that and this job, you're going to be in killer shape."

I put my hands on my hips. "I thought you liked the shape I was in right now."

He laughed and looked down, scraping his fingers through his close-cropped hair. "Oh, crap. Open mouth, insert foot." He beckoned me with a finger.

"Yes?" I asked with a raised brow, approaching him.

He pulled me to him and my heart began to race.

Shit. I knew I shouldn't encourage him, but every fiber in my body was begging for it.

He smoothed his hand over my ass. "You are perfect just as you are, Stell."

Oh my god. I hadn't been expecting that. "Thank you, Maze. That's very sweet."

He hooked a finger under my chin and forced me to look at him. "I think I see you blushing."

Ugh. Busted.

I rolled my eyes and wriggled out of his hold. "I have work to do, mister. I will not fall victim to your charms," I laughed.

"Ha. See if you can resist me," he called after me as I wheeled my bike to the back.

THE CROWD WAS STARTING to build, which thrilled me to no end. Not only did being busy make the time fly, but it also meant I stood to make some real money since the guys shared their tips.

Maze and I were behind the bar that night, and we were really in the flow. And for some reason, even the shitty parts of the job, like dealing with dirty drink glasses, weren't bothering me.

Maze had said I could make even more money if I tried bartending. He invited me to join his class. I was tempted. It would be a quick path to some serious cash. But I wanted to stay on track with my yoga teacher training, which was starting soon.

When I had plans, I stuck to them. Or tried to.

"Hey, Stell," Maze said, leaning toward me. "There's a guy at the end of the bar who's asking for you."

What? I didn't know anyone in Denver.

Unless…

As soon as I spotted Vaughn staring me down, a wine glass slipped out of my hand, crashing to the floor.

Dammit.

"You okay, Stell?" Maze asked.

He must have seen the look on my face, because he instantly realized something was up.

"Stell, who is that? What's wrong?"

I clenched my fists. That fucker was not only still in town, but he also had the nerve to come to my place of work.

"That's my ex. The guy I left behind in Philly."

Maze's eyebrows shot up. "No shit. Let me go get rid of him—unless you want to talk to him?"

I looked up at him with pleading eyes. "Get rid of him. Please."

I kept loading the bar's dishwasher but watched the guys out of the corner of my eye. Whatever exchange they had seemed pleasant enough and Vaughn left without a fuss.

"I told him you were too busy to socialize. He was cool about it," Maze said.

Hmmm. Vaughn was never cool about anything.

"Thanks, Maze. I appreciate it."

But I knew that wasn't the end of him.

As suspected, the night flew by in a blur. I was wiping down the bar for what I hoped was the last time, trying to keep myself from staring at Maze's sexy forearms, when an old familiar voice made my blood curdle.

"Hello, Stell."

I took a moment to look up. I didn't want to believe Vaughn had come back, and I thought if I didn't actually set eyes on him, then maybe the voice wasn't real.

But it was.

"What are you doing here? I thought Maze told you to leave," I hissed.

He gave me his smarmy grin. "Yeah. Your boyfriend told me to hit the road. Fuck that jerk."

"Fuck what jerk?" Maze asked, appearing at my side and placing a protective arm around my shoulder.

"I'd like to speak with Stell in private," Vaughn snapped.

Maze looked to me. "Stell. Why don't you tell us how you feel about that? You want to be alone with this man to have a conversation, or would you like me to stick around?"

I just looked up at him and before I could say anything, he answered for us both.

"It looks to me, my friend, that Stell doesn't want to speak with you, either alone or with me nearby. So you should probably hit the road," Maze said calmly. "Do you think you could do that?"

Vaughn laughed, trying to gain the upper hand.

He didn't know yet that he wouldn't be able to.

"Look, buddy," he started, shaking his finger, "you need to stay away from Stell. Keep your hands off her." He pointed to Maze's arm on my shoulder.

"Really?" Maze laughed. "I think Stell can make her own decisions. Like the decision she made about dumping your ass right before your wedding."

Rage turned Vaughn's eyes narrow and dark. "Do you know, *bartender*, who Stell's father is?"

"Why would I give a shit who Stell's father was?"

"You would if you were smart. He's a US congressman running for reelection. That means he'll stop at nothing to keep his reputation clean. Think about it. How do you think he'll feel when the press gets ahold of a photo of his daughter dirty dancing in your club, and then getting knocked over in a fight?"

Shit.

In a flash, Maze jumped over the bar and grabbed Vaughn by the front of his shirt. "I told you, fucker, to get out of my club and stay out. I'm done talking."

Vaughn's eyes grew wide, his bravado of a moment earlier vanishing. He clearly hadn't thought through what might happen when he pushed Maze too far.

Maze dragged Vaughn to the front door and shoved him out. "I don't want this fucker back in here," he shouted at the bouncers.

He returned to his spot behind the bar and started slamming things around.

"Um, thank you, Maze," I said.

He slammed a bottle of whiskey on the bar, the adrenaline still rolling. "I fucking hate guys like that."

Well. That made two of us.

29

Stell

"Oh my god, Cab, this place is insane."

I stood at a vast bay window with views toward the mountains.

Breathtaking was the only word for it.

"Check out the outside," he called from the kitchen where he was stirring a large pot of something that smelled amazing.

I pulled on a sliding glass door and stepped onto a wood-decked terrace lined with built-in seating and huge potted cactuses. In the middle was a sparkly fire pit and a far corner held a hot tub.

Oh. My. God.

"Isn't it great?" Robbie said, who'd just arrived.

"Hey, you're here," I said, as he kissed me on the cheek.

Sweet.

"Yup. So is Maze. I think he's pouring wine."

"How's baby Jax?" I asked.

Robbie adjusted his glasses as he transformed into a softer, happier version of himself. "He's awesome. So great." He shook his head like he couldn't believe his good fortune.

It was beautiful to see.

"Oh, hey, Cab's putting dinner on the table. Let's go," he said, letting me pass through the door first. "He's a killer cook."

"Hey, baby," Maze said, embracing me.

Baby? I was baby now?

We settled around Cab's giant rough-hewn dining table and dove into the roast chicken he'd made.

"Oh my god, Cab. Delicious." I hadn't realized how hungry I was.

Where had he learned to cook? Not growing up, that was for sure. His family had a freaking chef.

After a couple minutes of stuffing our faces, Maze broke the silence.

"Stell, I filled the guys in about Vaughn. If he gives you any more trouble let us know. We'll take care of it."

"You'll take care of it? What does that mean?" I asked.

Maybe I didn't want to know.

"Don't worry about the details, darlin'," Robbie said.

"But we'll make sure he leaves you alone, even if he has to learn the hard way."

"Wow. Thanks, guys."

Their promise was comforting, but also made me nervous. I didn't want anyone going too far.

Whatever 'too far' meant.

"There's something else we wanted to discuss with you," Maze said when we were nearly finished.

Um. Okay. I'd been wondering why I'd been invited for dinner with the three of them. Aside from the obvious reasons.

"I mentioned the other day about sharing," Cab said.

Like I could forget.

I nodded slowly, looking at each guy one at a time. God, they were fucking beautiful. And they were all looking right back at me, with pretty serious expressions.

"Right. But I'm still not sure what that means."

"You would be with all of us, darlin'," Robbie said. "We'd share you. It's our thing."

I still didn't get it, and I suppose confusion was written all over my face from the way the guys reacted.

"For one thing, you know I'm on my way to LA—" I started to say.

Maze held his hands up. "Stell, you like Denver. You could consider sticking around. You could get your yoga teacher certificate, and work at the bar once in a while if you wanted to when we had parties and stuff."

They wanted me to stick around? *That* I was not

expecting. I also wasn't expecting the fluttery feeling in my stomach that followed.

"Um, geez. I'm... flattered."

My thoughts wandered back to the other night when we'd all been together.

Yum.

Not knowing what else to do, I stood and began removing empty plates from the table. But as I came around the corner of the table, Cab took my hand and brought it to his lips.

Tilting his head, he smiled at me. "I gotta tell you guys, this woman was beautiful when we were growing up, but she's even more beautiful now."

"Oh my god. Shut up," I said, play-smacking him.

"I believe it, man," Robbie said, jumping to his feet. "C'mon, darlin'. Put the dishes down. Let's get more comfortable."

Well then.

Our fingers intertwined, I followed him to the living room, all rustic with exposed beams and a stone fireplace taking up almost an entire wall. The sofas and chairs were laden with fluffy throw pillows, and a cowhide rug covered the floor.

I did a three-sixty to take it all in. "I love it."

As I finished, Robbie placed his hands on the sides of my face, having removed his glasses to reveal the same eyes his baby boy had.

"Wow is right," he said, pressing his forehead against mine and closing his eyes.

I fell into him. I wanted to forget the Vaughn bullshit and just feel. And I was on my way.

I pressed my lips to Robbie's, while two hands wandered under my shirt from behind. When they reached my breasts, they pushed my bra aside and rubbed my nipples until they were hard and aching.

Robbie took a step back to unbutton my blouse, and when it had fallen to the floor, he smiled. "Look at those tits."

"Indeed," Cab said as he pulled my hard points.

Maze appeared on my left. "Such a special girl. So pretty, smart, and gutsy."

Here I was with the three guys again and I was pretty sure I'd died and gone to heaven. Or if I hadn't, I sure hoped heaven was like this.

I reached for Maze. I needed to kiss him just like I had Robbie. He was protective.

They were all protective. And it felt so good.

I'd known these guys only a short period of time, and yet their kindness had created such a deep connection between us. I wanted it to grow.

Even if I knew it might not be a wise thing to do.

While I kissed Maze, Cab removed my bra and Robbie relieved me of my blue jeans. His fingers slipped inside my sheer panties to run through my wet folds.

It felt so fucking good.

I reached for Maze's belt and had it and his trousers open in seconds. I fumbled through a tangle of boxers and wrapped my fingers around his big, rigid cock, the one I'd held just a couple nights before.

"Oh, that feels nice, baby," he murmured against my lips.

I had to have my mouth on him. I dropped to my knees and held him by the root. There was a small drop of precum on the tip of his head and I rubbed it on my lips, licking him clean.

"You like the taste of my cum?" he said in a deep, scratchy voice.

"Mmmm." I pulled him in my mouth until he hit the back of my throat.

"Holy fuck," Cab said.

I stopped long enough to open Robbie's and Cab's jeans to get to their cocks. As soon as they were in my hands, I wrapped my lips around Maze again and sucked him with the same rhythm I was stroking the guys.

I had all three of their cocks thrusting at me, in and out of my hands and mouth. It felt so damn dirty and so damn good. They looked down at me in wonder, and I felt beautiful and powerful.

"I want to be inside you," Robbie said. "Can I fuck you, darlin'?"

My mouth full, I nodded. Maze pulled out long enough to lie back on the rug. This left me on my hands and knees and someone's fingers reached under me to rub my clit.

I closed my eyes. There were three pair of hands

wandering all over my body in the most mind-blowing way.

Robbie sheathed himself with a condom and got on his knees behind me, gripping my hips with his huge hands. It was so dominant, the way he was taking what he wanted, with me on my knees with my legs spread and ass raised, offering my pussy.

He entered me slowly, spreading my wet excitement up and down his cock. When he was completely slick, he drove all the way inside, pushing me toward Maze, whose cock was in my mouth.

"Jesus, baby, I think I'm halfway down your throat," he murmured, rocking his hips.

With my mouth and pussy full, all I could do was buck back and forth, first taking Maze and then Robbie as deeply as possible.

"Fuck, look at you guys tag teaming our girl," Cab breathed as he alternately played with my tits, then my clit, and then my tits again.

"Oh, Christ," Maze groaned, stiffening even harder and then filling my mouth with his warm cum.

"Yeah, suck him, Stell," Robbie growled behind me. "I love watching you do that. It's gonna make me come too." He rammed me one last time, pushing me over my own edge. I bucked against him and an orgasm hit me like a tsunami, while he emptied himself at the same time.

When both guys pulled out of me, we all collapsed onto the floor to catch our breath. The guys lay around me, all holding me somewhere on my body so we were connected like a large pod.

"Guys, that was incredible," I said, my heart still pounding. "You're so amazing."

"No, we're not," Cab said quietly. "You are the amazing one."

30

Robbie

"ROBBIE? Robbie, I've been calling you."

It was six in the fucking morning. Who calls a bartender at six in the morning?

But I didn't have to wonder for more than a second. I'd know that voice if it were thousands of miles away.

"Good morning to you too, Elise."

Jax cooed in the background and I heard the rustling of her shifting him from one arm to the other.

"And what do you mean, you've been calling me? I don't have a single message from you," I said, sitting up in the bed I'd grabbed in Cab's guest room.

His place was dead silent. No doubt I was the only one awake after our hot night with Stell.

"Why are you speaking so quietly, Robbie?" she demanded. "You got a girl over? Someone else you're going to impregnate?"

Really?

"Maze and I spent the night at Cab's and I'm pretty certain they're still asleep, like I wish I were."

I didn't bother to mention Stell.

"We need to meet, Robbie."

"Fine. Is everything okay?"

She scoffed. "Sure. Everything is great. I've been up half the night because Jax preferred to play rather than sleep."

She acted like she was the only one kept up by a baby. I had him half the time, too. But I didn't bother to point it out, because I didn't see it as a burden.

Being Jax's father was something I looked at as more of a privilege.

"I want Jax full-time," she said.

Huh? Wasn't she just bitching about being sleep deprived?

"Elise, you know that's not possible. We share custody of him. What's behind this?"

Silence.

"Elise. Talk to me. What's up?"

"My mom is moving to Arizona. If I go with her, she'll take care of Jax during the day."

Yeah, I don't think so.

"Well, I think it's generous of your mom to offer to help, but you're not taking Jax to Arizona."

Things slammed around in the background. "Fuck you, Robbie. I know what's best for my baby, and he doesn't deserve to be brought up by a degenerate father who runs a bar."

Since when was I a degenerate? And I didn't just run a bar. I was part-owner in the biggest club in Denver.

But I could see what she was doing, clear as day. She'd thought this through, and this was the beginning of her making a case against me.

Which was not going to happen.

"I have a lawyer," she blurted out, like that was going to intimidate me.

I took a deep breath. I didn't want Stell or the guys to hear me arguing. "You're not taking him to Arizona, Elise. I won't allow it. And I don't care how many lawyers you have, or how bad you try to make me look. It won't work. The court won't award you full custody if I don't agree."

"Fine. You'll hear from my lawyer then. And expect it to be expensive."

She hung up.

What a way to wake up. Now there was no way I was getting back to sleep.

She'd never get full custody of Jax, but keeping that from happening could be costly. Elise had her mother's large bank account to finance her whims. It was a different story for me.

I did have money in the bank, of course, and I could

sell my sports car for something more practical like a used SUV. It would certainly be easier to cart Jax around in a full-sized, grown up vehicle.

I texted one of my buddies who sold cars.

know anyone who might want to buy my Porsche?

Since I knew I wasn't going back to sleep, I started reading the news on my phone before I switched over to researching custody issues. I had to do something. It would be hours before everybody else woke up.

In order to get Cab's old man off our back, we stepped up our private parties. In the past, we'd kept them to a minimum because one, they were a lot of work, and two, we wanted them to seem exclusive. But our needs had changed, and we began to say yes more often than we said no.

Actually, our amazing bookkeeper and general operations person, Deb, was the one saying yes or no. I stayed out of events. I was not a details guy. It was all I could do to remember to bring a diaper with me every time I had the little man.

We'd asked Stell to work tonight's party with us. She and I were setting up a small bar in the Playroom when I noticed Deb was still in the office.

"Hey there. Thank you for setting these parties up. I'm sure when you took the bookkeeping position you didn't realize you'd also become an event planner."

She laughed. "I actually like it. It's fun. Well, mostly fun. Some of the people who want to have parties here are pretty freaking sketch."

I knew that to be the truth. But Deb had grown up in Denver and knew a shit ton of people. She could usually do some recon and find out all we needed to know about whether someone was going to throw a fairly manageable party, or attract troublemakers.

"All I can say, Deb, is that you are a godsend."

She smiled at me and got back to work.

Loved that woman.

And there was our lovely Stell, arranging bottles on the portable bar, or 'party bar', as she called it, in the order we liked so we could grab them and make drinks quickly.

She was especially gorgeous in a low-cut blouse that, when she moved just the right way, revealed a wisp of her black lace bra. She'd gathered her hair at the back of her neck in a messy little knot, which was so different from the braids or ponytails she wore during a regular work night.

By any measure, she was a breathtaking woman, but with the extra effort she'd made for tonight's party, I couldn't keep my eyes off her.

And couldn't stop thinking of the hot freaking time we had together at Cab's the night before.

I'd hoped she'd respond to us the way she had. I'm not sure it was wishful thinking from the first time I'd met her at our car accident, or just her plucky, take-no-shit attitude, but she'd turned out to be as passionate as I expected her to be. And then some.

I also hoped she'd decide to stick around Denver, if not permanently, then at least for a long, long time. But if her heart was set on LA, then of course that was where she should go.

One thing I knew, was that whatever she decided, we'd support her. What was best for her was best for us all. We weren't about holding women back just because it suited our needs or desires.

"Robbie," Stell called, gesturing me over, "why is Annabel here? Is she waitressing for the party?"

Oh, shit. She was always trouble and Maze was procrastinating on firing her.

She saw us looking at her and headed our way. "Hey, guys," she said, tying on her apron.

"Annabel, I didn't know you were working tonight. Is your name on the schedule?" I asked.

My mind was racing trying to think of a way to get rid of her. We didn't really need waitresses for parties. If they were of a manageable enough size, folks could get their drinks at the small bar.

She smiled coyly. "Oh. Well, I wasn't on the schedule. But Hayley asked me to swap shifts with her."

Swap shifts, my ass. Hayley never gave up shifts, especially not for a private party, which was always lucrative for the staff.

I sighed. "How much did you pay her, Annabel?" I asked.

She put her hand on her chest. "What? Nothing. I didn't pay her anything. She um... wanted to trade." She turned on her heel and headed into the growing crowd.

I got behind the bar with Stell, and while I was annoyed as hell with Annabel, I was cheered by the woman next to me. And I wasn't sure whether it was perfume or just nice lotion, but her scent was lovely and reminded me of last night.

My brain wasn't the only thing remembering. I had to shift myself in my blue jeans to avoid ending up in agony.

Stell set up the glasses for a round of muddled drinks as I pulled out the herbs we needed.

"You look very pretty tonight, Stell," I said.

She flashed her amazing smile. I wanted to kiss her lips so badly I wasn't sure I could wait until the end of the night.

Thirty minutes later, the party was in full swing. The crowd was a good-looking one with the women dressed to kill and the men appreciating their efforts. The DJ got going and there was a lot of sexy gyrating on the dance floor. In one dark corner were two women and one man, clearly getting to know each other better. It wouldn't be the first time a party in the Playroom was rated R.

Or even X.

An empty glass slammed onto the bar.

Both Stell and I snapped our heads in the direction of the noise. Trouble already?

Yup. But unfortunately, the trouble was not one of our guests. It was an employee.

Annabel. Because of course.

She gestured to the corner where the threesome was bumping and grinding. "That is disgusting. Are you going to let this sort of thing happen in your club?"

Stell grabbed the glass out of Annabel's hands so she couldn't throw it. "They're just kissing. Who gives a damn? If you don't like it, Annabel, don't look."

Or better yet, go home.

Which I was inches away from telling her.

She screwed up her face in anger. "I wasn't talking to you, *bar girl*."

Stell rolled her eyes and tried not to laugh.

I loved that about her. Oh shit. Did I say *love?*

"Robbie, do you want it known that you have *orgies* here at Tableau?" she spat, her eyes bloodshot with indignation.

I took a deep breath to keep my calm. I doubted it was going to work, though.

"Annabel, maybe this isn't the kind of party you should be working. Why don't you head home? I think Stell and I can handle things from here."

I didn't bother telling her Maze would be here later. She'd never leave if she thought she might see him.

"Fuck you, Robbie," she exploded.

She reached behind the bar, and threw a glass that barely missed Stell, who'd ducked just in time.

31

Robbie

"What the...?" Stell hollered.

The psycho had really pissed me off now.

"Okay, Annabel," I said, grabbing her arm and directing her toward the door, "you're fired. It's been a long time coming, and this is the last straw."

But before I could get her out of the party, she turned to the crowd and screamed, "Whores!"

Most of the people ignored her, but a few turned their heads in her direction and laughed.

She struggled in my grip but was no match for me as I half-dragged her down the stairs and to the club's front door. When we reached it, I pushed her outside.

"This woman doesn't work here anymore," I told

the bouncer. "And she's not welcome as a customer, either."

Our burly doorman looked her up and down and nodded. "Sure thing, boss."

Wow. We should have done that long ago.

I took the stairs back up two at a time, knowing people were waiting for their drinks. But both Maze and Cab had arrived and had already gotten to work keeping our customers' thirst quenched.

"Did you guys come in the back door?" I asked.

"Yup. And we just heard about Annabel. Stell told us," Cab said, nodding in her direction.

I scraped my hair back into the usual ponytail-bun I wore at work. "You're lucky. You just missed her. She's gone, guys. And good riddance."

Stell shook her head, dumping the broken glass she'd swept up into the trash. "That woman is a mess. I feel for her."

We looked at Stell. Leave it to her to remind us to look at someone like Annabel with compassion.

"You're right, baby," Maze said, giving her a kiss on the temple.

I watched to see how she'd react to being kissed in semi-public. Her eyes darted around the room, and when she realized that no one gave a shit, she popped him a kiss on the cheek.

That's my girl.

"Hey, if you want to take a break, Stell. I've got things under control," Maze said.

She wiped her hands on her apron. "Good idea. I think I'll do that."

Cab and I exchanged looks. "Want some company?"

Her eyes widened, and a slow smile crept across her face. "Yes. I would love some company."

Maze laughed, and continued pouring champagne, while Cab took one of Stell's hands, and I took the other.

32

Stell

I COULDN'T LIE. All the bumping and grinding at the party had gotten me hot and bothered. It was one sexy crowd we were hosting—both the men and the women.

And when Maze and Cab arrived, and I had all the guys right there in front of me, looking at me with desire, there was no holding back.

I had a hundred reasons to say no, and only one to say yes.

Plain and simple, I wanted them, and that was a good enough reason for me.

I wanted their hands all over my body like they had been the night before. In fact, I wanted it so badly I'd been thinking about it all day. I'd never felt so able to ask for what I wanted sexually and because of that I wanted everything.

I wanted it *all* and I wanted it *now*.

So much *want*.

I led the guys to the lounge area on the mezzanine, which was dark and quiet since the party we were hosting was confined to the Playroom.

The mezzanine was usually filled with the club's high rollers who ordered bottle service and other obscenely overpriced things like cigars that they had to go outside to smoke. It was a see-and-be-seen kind of groove and because I was always working, I'd never had the chance to hang out there.

Not that anyone was inviting me, anyway.

But tonight I had free run of the club and wanted to take full advantage of it.

I looked over the mezzanine railing to the floor below. "It must be wild to be up here when the club's in full swing. Music blaring, and you're just looking down on all the sweaty, writhing bodies. Like a king looking down on his subjects."

Cab's hand wrapped around my waist from behind and he nuzzled my neck. "Or a queen looking down on *her* subjects."

And my knees felt weak.

His hand slipped up over my blouse and he gripped one of my breasts. Robbie appeared on my right and turned me to brush his lips against mine.

I say brush, because he wasn't exactly kissing me.

He was teasing me. Like giving me a little taste of dinner before it was ready, when I was hungry as a starving animal.

"Baby, I want to taste your pussy," Cab murmured in my ear.

Okay. I'd thought my knees were already weak, but now? I had to hold the mezzanine railing to keep from collapsing into a puddle of inarticulate, stark raving mad need.

"Come with me, darlin'," Robbie said, leading me by the hand.

He and Cab took seats on the sofa, relaxing with their hands behind their heads.

I stood before them.

"What are you waiting for?" Robbie asked.

I pointed at myself. "Me? What do you mean?"

He rolled his eyes impatiently. "Undress."

Oh. Gotcha.

The Playroom's music drifted in our direction, inspiring me to swivel my hips while I unbuttoned the top of my blouse. I moved on to my jeans, leaving them partly open, just enough to show my panties.

"That's what I'm talking about," Cab said, nodding.

I turned, and with my back to them, moved my hips in time to the music while I opened my blouse all the way. With a peek over my shoulder, I let the silky fabric slide down my back.

Robbie gave a low whistle, and he adjusted himself in his jeans.

I grabbed my blouse as it floated to the floor and tossed it in the guys' direction. I don't know who caught it because I'd already turned around and started unzipping my pants.

Inch by inch, I eased my tight jeans down and over my ass, keeping my silky thong in place. When my pants were all the way to the floor, I bent down to step out of them, making sure the guys got a good view of my ass and other goodies.

"Nice, baby," Cab growled.

Wearing only my bra and panties, I danced up to the guys, first rubbing my breasts in their faces, then shaking my ass. I'd never felt so sexy. Beautiful. Powerful. Desired.

"Lie back," Cab said, pointing at the coffee table in the middle of the room.

When I did, he pulled my thong down, tossed it aside, and pushed my knees far apart.

"Look at this pussy."

Robbie ran a finger through my wet folds, then slipped it inside, following with another. Cab placed his tongue on my clit, circling it at first and then sucking until I was writhing.

Both of these gorgeous men were working me over like I'd never been. I was in heaven. Robbie pumped me faster, and an orgasm took over. My head thrashed back and forth on the table and my hips bucked into Cab's mouth. I tried to keep my noise to a minimum, not wanting to attract unwanted attention.

Not sure how successful that was.

"Fuck, baby," Cab said when he finally gave my clit a rest. "I'm gonna slide a rubber on, and then I want you to hurry up and come sit on top of me over there on that sofa."

Who was I to argue?

Robbie helped me up, holding my hand as I wobbled over to Cab.

He hadn't been kidding when he said he wanted me to hurry. Before I knew it, he had his pants around his knees and was holding his huge cock at the base, the perfect angle for entering me.

I placed a knee on either side of his hips and hovered my pussy above him. With my hands on either side of his beautiful face, I reached down and pressed my lips to his. Kissing him was deliciously familiar, and also new at the same time. It had been a lifetime ago that we'd been together. We were just kids.

Now we were older. More experienced.

Sexier.

I ran my fingers through my slit, opening myself for him, then lowered until he was halfway in.

"You okay, baby?" he asked.

"Yeah. Oh god, yeah," I murmured into the crook of his neck.

He shifted his hips up and at the same time, lowered me until I was utterly impaled. I gripped his shoulders for purchase, digging my nails into him, and we moved together in a perfect rhythm. Robbie, who was behind me, pinched and pulled my nipples nearly to the point of causing me pain.

And I loved it.

"Come," Cab demanded. "I want you to come first so I can fuck the shit out of you."

I started moving a little faster. I reached down and fingered my clit, knowing that would push me over my edge. I didn't have to work for long because his big dick, stretching my walls to the limit, kicked off a vibrating hum spreading from my pussy to the ends of my four limbs. My spine arched involuntarily and I dropped my head back. I didn't recognize the moans coming from my own throat, I was out of it as I came over and over.

When I was so spent I couldn't move, I slumped forward onto Cab, who put his hands under my ass, picked me up, and lay me back on the sofa to change position. I turned to look at Robbie, who was stroking himself, and I pulled him to my mouth.

Meanwhile, Cab opened my legs and positioned himself between them. "Are you ready, baby?" he asked.

"I am, Cab. Fuck me. Hard."

Before the words were completely out of my mouth, he'd rammed himself so deeply inside me I nearly flew off the sofa. I reached for Robbie, who I was sucking hard, for something to hold on to.

Cab drove into me again and again while I swallowed Robbie, the three of us moving together in a perfect rhythm.

The only thing missing was Maze.

With a loud bellow, Cab exploded inside me, pumping until he had nothing left. He pulled out just in time to see Robbie come all over my tits.

We were quiet for a second, when we heard a giggle.

Robbie tucked himself back in his pants and looked over the edge of the mezzanine to the floor below.

"Don't mind us," a female voice called. "We were just enjoying listening."

Robbie laughed and made his way back over to help me get dressed.

"Want to stay over at my place tonight?" Cab asked.

I'd gathered his condo was the de facto guys' clubhouse, and that while the other two had their own places, they frequently gathered at the one with the views and the hot tub.

I couldn't blame them.

"I'd love to. Will you come too, Robbie?" I asked.

He broke out in a huge grin as he put his glasses back on. "Shit. What do you think, I'm an idiot?"

Stell

I COULDN'T BELIEVE I was doing what I was about to do. It was unfathomable.

But I had some weird, sad, convoluted hope that if I talked to Vaughn one last time in person, he might get some closure and go back to his life in Philly.

And most importantly, get out of my damn hair.

"You look nice," he said, joining me at the corner table I'd snagged in Starbucks. "Can I get you anything?"

I pointed to my latte. "Already took care of it."

That's because he was thirty minutes late. Like always.

"Oh. Right. Sorry I'm late."

As I faced him, all I could think about was how lucky I was that he cheated on me, and that I met the guys. My handsome, sexy guys.

"How long are you staying in Denver?" I asked, turning slightly in my chair to avoid his overly intense gaze.

There was a time when I would have been tickled by that. But no more.

"I'm here until I can convince you to come back with me to Philly." He sat back in his seat, like my joining him was a foregone conclusion.

Asshole.

"Vaughn, maybe you should have thought of that before you let Suza suck your dick."

The smile melted from his face and he leaned onto the table to make his point. "I made a mistake. I'm sorry. I was... nervous about getting married. It was a terrible thing to do."

I thought back to the photo of him with his hand up another woman's skirt. I'd always wondered who was behind it. Not that it mattered. What did was that he was busted, and I avoided making a terrible mistake.

"It seems you think your driving cross country to see me to apologize assumes I give a shit, and that I would consider our being a couple again."

He shrugged. "Well, of course. I mean, what the hell else do you want?"

Bam.

What *did* I want? Excellent question. And I felt like I was getting closer to clarity on that every day.

I was losing my patience. "I can tell you want I *don't* want, and that is *you.*"

He pressed his lips together. At this point a normal person would graciously give up and go away. But not Vaughn, the entitled fuck.

So I decided to make it crystal clear. "What you don't seem to comprehend is that I want nothing to do with you. Ever. I think you are a disgusting excuse for a man, and I thank my lucky stars I confirmed your terrible personality problems before it was too late."

He smiled smugly, nodding slowly, looking out Starbucks' window at the passersby.

Then he turned back to me. "Look. We *belong* together."

"No, Vaughn, we don't—"

He held his hands up and cut me off. "I feel so strongly about this that I'm willing to go to great lengths to get you back to Philly. Starting with sharing the photo I have of you doing your little dirty dancing thing."

Fuck. I'd thought that was off the table. But I guess when you're desperate, you'll try anything.

I spoke slowly to remain calm, but the truth was that if I'd had something sharp, it would have been poking out of his chest at that very moment.

"Why do you want me so badly you'll do anything

to get me back? Why would you want to be with someone who hates you?" I asked.

I had a feeling I knew what was coming next.

"You come from a good family. You're a nice girl."

And there it was. He wanted to have a congressman for a father-in-law for whatever benefit it might bring him.

He clearly wasn't going away easily, and I had to come up with something drastic. I needed to buy some time and to talk to the guys. They'd offered to help me, and it was time to call in that favor.

I took a deep breath to prepare for the line of bull-shit I was about to deliver. "All right, Vaughn. Give me some time. I need to think about it. Get used to the idea. My yoga instructor training starts tomorrow and goes for two weeks. I'll finish that and then maybe go back to Philly. Are you okay with my staying that long?"

I wanted to throw up. Placating this creep did not come naturally.

He sat back in his chair, arms crossed, like he'd achieved a victory.

If he only knew.

"I guess we could do that."

Big of him.

"I want you to stay with me at my hotel."

Wow. He really was delusional.

"No. I'm… not ready for that. I'll stay where I am, with Marni."

He rolled his eyes. "I've never understood how you could stand her. She's such a bitch."

Ha. I knew he was jealous of my friendship with her. I *knew* it.

"Well, she never had a bad thing to say about you. Until you... fucked up, that is."

An expression passed over his face that I couldn't quite define, but that let me know he didn't like being reminded of his wrongdoing.

Tough shit.

I looked at my watch and stood. "Gotta go."

He looked me up and down like I was his property.

Dick.

"I'm glad we made progress today. I really am, Stell. I'll never do anything like that again."

Didn't matter to me. The bastard was never going to get the chance.

❧

"Oh my god, Marn. Can you talk?"

"Sure. What's up?"

The sounds of the gym filled the background.

"First, I got my car back."

I couldn't lie any longer. And riding a bike had gotten old.

"Great," she said.

"Also, I just had coffee with Vaughn."

She gasped. "Really? Why?"

"I thought I could get him off my back. Talk some sense into him. But no go. He says if I don't go back to Philly with him, he'll expose some photos he has of me dancing on the platform at Tableau."

A door clicked, and I knew she'd gone into a private office. "Oh crap. How did he get those?"

"I don't know. He must have sneaked in somehow."

She exhaled a loud breath, and after a moment, spoke. "You know, Stell. What's the worst that can happen if he goes public with that? Who cares? You're a grown woman and can dance wherever you want."

If only it were that easy.

"But Marn, you know my dad is up for reelection."

She was silent for a moment. "I know. And I know this will sound kind of cold, but that's not your problem. You have your own life to live."

"They'd never forgive me."

I could see it now. Drama of the nuclear variety.

"So what? Seriously, Stell. You're out on your own now. If they're so willing to write you off for living your life, is theirs a club worth belonging to?"

Damn.

I loved that about Marni. She always helped me see through the dark. But I had a lot to think about. If I left the club of Mom and Dad, what club would I then belong to?

I had a couple ideas.

34

Cab

"MARN, you won't believe the bullshit Dad is pulling."

I filled her in while she swirled a teabag around her cup, slowly shaking her head in disbelief. "Unfucking-believable. Maybe I can talk to him."

It was sweet of her to offer. But that sexist old man had no interest in advice from any woman, much less his daughter. He loved Marni, but looked at her as a sort of pretty accessory who he was happy to invest in until she married and started squeezing out babies.

"Thanks, Marn. But I think that would make things worse. You know how he is with women."

With a faraway look in her eyes, her gaze wandered

over the as-yet empty club. It was early yet, but the crowds would start showing up soon.

"I wonder if he's gonna pull the plug on me and the gym at some point?"

God, I hoped not. That would break Marni's heart. She'd worked her fingers to the bone on Altitude, and she'd surpassed all her goals for membership and revenues. She was a smart cookie and could actually run any business she wanted to.

"He might, Marn. I don't say that to be a dick. It's just reality."

She looked stricken at the thought, but shook it off. "You know, I have some money saved up. How much do you need?"

"In order to keep Dad from selling Tableau, we'd have to completely buy him out. Once he no longer had a financial interest in the club, he'd have no hold over me."

I leaned on the bar, closer to my sister. I didn't need any patrons knowing about my financial woes. "I need a quarter of a million dollars. I know that sounds crazy, but it's do-able if I can buy some time. Our private parties are ten grand and above. If we did one or two a week, we'd have enough money to buy him out in a few months. Thing is, I'm not sure he's giving me that long. You don't happen to have a quarter million bucks, do you?" I asked with a weak laugh.

"Um, no. I do not have that kind of money," she said.

Shit, shit, shit.

She patted my hand. "So, on another subject, you seem to be having fun with Stell. Just like old times, huh?"

Not a moment went by that I didn't thank my lucky stars the lovely Stell had reappeared in my life. She might not be in it for long if she decided to take off for LA, but for the time that she was here, I planned to revel in her company.

"I am having fun with her. All us guys are," I said, thinking back to the last time she sucked my dick. "Marn, I feel so bad about what I did to her."

Hell, if there wasn't a lump stuck in my throat. And I was at goddamn work.

My sister looked at me and was silent. There really wasn't much to say. I'd fucked up.

"Well," she said quietly, "you were young and Dad manipulated you."

Still. If I'd had any balls, I'd have told him to fuck off.

"Why does he hate Stell's dad so much, anyway?" I said.

I'd grown up knowing there was bad blood between my father and Congressman Kline, which became even more awkward when Marni and Stell became friends. But to get in the way of a budding romance? That was seriously shitty.

Marni took a deep breath. "I think it might have to do with—a very long time ago—some sort of affair."

I'd figured as much. The Congressman was not known for being faithful to his wife. I didn't know who fucked whom, and I didn't want to know.

"Crazy shit," I said, shaking my head.

Marni reached across the bar and touched my cheek. She knew better than anyone how I'd suffered over what I'd done, and the pain it had inflicted on Stell. And yet she never took sides.

She smiled slyly. "Does she know yet about... your sharing thing? She hasn't really mentioned much to me. I want to wait for her to feel comfortable talking about it all."

I nodded, watching a band of frat bros filter in, raising hell like they owned the place. They probably weren't going to last the night. They'd get kicked out long before closing. I'd seen it so often I could tell in advance who was going to behave and who wasn't.

"We have... broached the subject. Understandably, at first she was a little taken aback. Shit, maybe she still is. We asked her to stay here in Denver. I hope she does."

Marni tapped her fingers on the bar. "Speaking of Stell, she shared with me that Vaughn was still harassing her."

"You're kidding me. We bounced that creep out of here on his ass and warned him to leave her alone."

Goddammit. My mood shifted from just plain crummy, thanks to my dad, to downright shitty, thanks to Vaughn.

"He's threatening to go to the press with a photo of her dancing on the platform. I told her not to worry about it. She did nothing wrong. She's a freaking adult. But you know how dutiful she is."

I scowled and I had a feeling I would continue to all night. "When you're brought up surrounded by an obsessive preoccupation with what your family's public image is, I guess it's hard to let that go."

"It doesn't help that her dad's up for reelection." Marni looked at her watch and stood. "Anyway, I gotta get over to the gym and take care of some paperwork. And from the looks of the girls down at the end of the bar, you're going to be having fun making a lot of fruity drinks."

Holy shit. Was that another bachelorette party? Jesus. Was everyone in Denver getting married?

But making frou-frou drinks was the least of my worries. I needed to talk to the guys and set in motion a plan to get that asshole Vaughn off Stell's back.

And my shit mood was getting shittier by the moment. Stell was at her yoga teacher class, so I was stuck with a busboy helping me out behind the bar. He was a good guy and worked hard, but he didn't have the eye for anticipating things like Stell did.

It was funny. A congressman's daughter who turned out to be a top-notch barback, lugging ice and washing dirty cocktail glasses. And never complaining about it. Instead, she just worked harder. I doubted Congressman Kline had any idea. Knowing Stell, she'd probably not told her parents a thing about her latest job.

In fact, she'd probably not even told them she and I were back in touch. I knew from Marni that when I left town at my father's direction, Stell was upset and because of that, so were her parents.

They probably hated me just like she did. Thank god I'd turned that situation around. All those years of guilt might someday be erased by the opportunity to treat Stell with the respect she deserved. If I could forgive myself. I wanted to, but wasn't sure I didn't deserve to hate that part of myself. I'd done a terrible thing and I'd do anything for redemption.

Since I couldn't get her off my mind, I shot her a text.

hey. why don't you come by the club to say hi when you're done with yoga?

sure. I might be sweaty, though

Sweaty? Bring it on. I didn't care how sweaty she was, as long as she was close by. The closer the better.

Now I had something to look forward to as I made probably my fiftieth Sex on the Beach shooter of the night. Concerns about my father and the jerk-off Vaughn certainly weren't gone, but they took less out of me knowing I'd see Stell soon.

35

Cab

AND LIKE CLOCKWORK, my girl breezed in, her hair piled on top of her head, her face red from the exertion of class. She radiated happiness, and was more stunning than ever.

"Hi," she said when she'd squeezed up to the bar and finagled a seat.

I leaned over and kissed her. I couldn't help it.

"What can I get you, beautiful?"

She blushed. She actually blushed.

"Club soda would be great, thanks."

I delivered her beverage and got back to work making twenty dollar muddled drinks for a couple women, and pouring a round of beers for the frat group. They'd attracted the attention of one of our bouncers, which didn't bode well for them.

I finally had a minute to breathe. "Stell, I heard Vaughn is back in the picture. Marni filled me in."

Time to put an end to this bullshit once and for all.

She rolled her eyes and nodded. "I don't know what to do. I actually considered for a split second caving and going back with him. You know, the path of least resistance."

My stomach dropped. Holy fuck. That was the last thing she should be doing.

"So what *are* you going to do?" I asked, trying to sound casual, the words strangling in my throat.

"I hate that guy. I'm not going anywhere with him." Whew.

She waved her hand as if it would make thoughts of him go away. "Hey, different subject. I saw Annabel outside in the parking lot. She was crying, saying she missed Maze."

Oh, shit. She was worse off than we'd thought.

"Were they ever together, like she claims?" Stell asked. "Like as a couple?"

"No. Maze says they kissed once, and that's when it started, her imagining there was more going on than there really was."

I felt for Annabel. The woman clearly needed help. But I was also a bit concerned about her mental stability, or lack of it.

"Cab, I think I know how Vaughn got the picture of

me dancing," she said, pushing wisps of hair out of her face.

The wisps I wanted to be touching.

"I thought he just sneaked in somehow."

She nodded. "Yes, that's what I thought initially, but I talked to the security guys. They had a picture of him, so were on alert. He couldn't get in unless he could walk through the walls. I think he got Annabel to do it."

Holy shit.

"When I was talking to her earlier and she was going on and on about Maze, she asked when I was going back to Philly. There's no way she would know that, unless he told her."

So, *two* people we needed to watch out for.

"What are you gonna do about the photo?"

She took a deep breath. "I don't know yet."

"Hey, do you want to hang out and keep me company until we close tonight?" I asked.

A smile spread across her pretty face. "Maybe..." she said.

Ugh. What she did to me.

Time had never moved as slowly as when I was dying to get off work and wrap my arms around Stell. I kept my head down, served drinks like a bastard, and before I knew it the bouncers had chased the last person out of the club.

"Here. I'll help you clean up," Stell said, joining me behind the bar.

Like the champ that she was, she loaded dirty

glasses in the dishwasher, put away the booze bottles, and wiped down a busy night's worth of mess.

"Wow," I said, looking around the bar. "The place looks great. Guess I'm going to have to pay you for this work."

She sidled up to me, putting her arms around me while looking up at my face.

I could have stayed just like that, forever.

I leaned closer to her hair. "God, you smell so fucking good," I said.

"What do you say to going upstairs to the office?" she asked.

Like she didn't already know the answer.

I took her hand. "I think we should do that. I need to put the cash drawer in the safe, after all. Right now."

She giggled and we ran up the stairs to the office like happy little kids.

But we didn't act like kids once the office door was closed. And locked.

Stell jumped on me before I'd even set the cash drawer down, starting with yanking my shirt out of my pants, and reaching down them to grab my growing cock.

"Fuck baby, you're not wasting any time," I growled.

"We've wasted enough time. Like several years," she said, tearing at my belt and fly with one hand while the other was buried deep inside my jeans.

In seconds, my pants were around my ankles. She

kneeled before me, and took my cockhead between her lips, rolling it around and tasting my precum.

I wanted to shove myself down her throat and come, that's how fucking worked up I was, but I also wanted to see her come. So I held back.

She cupped my balls and slowly worked my dick into her mouth, holding the desk for balance with her free hand.

"Mmmm," she murmured with a full mouth.

I held her head while she began to piston me, moving my hips to her rhythm.

"Oh, fuck, baby," I roared. "I gotta stop. Let's stop for a sec. I don't want to come."

I pulled myself out of her mouth, leaving her with bright red lips from the friction, mascara pooled under her eyes, and saliva running down her chin.

I grabbed a condom out of the office's desk drawer and sheathed myself.

"Turn and face the desk," I commanded. "Put your hands on it."

I slipped her yoga pants below her ass and to her knees. Her legs, bound as they were by the stretchy fabric, kept her from parting them very far. But that was okay. I liked her bound.

"I'm gonna fuck you now, Stell. Are you ready?"

"Mmmm," was all she could say as she wagged her ass at me.

With my hands on her cheeks, I spread her open for a view of her pink asshole and juicy pussy. Someday I wouldn't mind trying anal with her, but I'd save that for another day.

I directed my dick to her slick opening. It slipped in easily, that's how ready she was for me.

"Give me more, Cab. I want it all," she whispered, lowering her head to the desk.

I drove myself balls-deep so hard her hands slipped on the desk, knocking piles of paper and other crap to the floor.

Did I care?

Fuck no.

"Oh god. I love it, I love it," she kept murmuring over and over.

I pistoned her slow at first and then faster until I was breathing so hard I thought I'd pass out. Stell gripped the desk like her life depended on it.

Her pussy clamped down on me, and her moans got louder. "I'm coming, Cab. I'm coming, now," she said, her breath hoarse and raspy.

She gasped, her screams turning into incoherent mumbling. I closed my eyes, lost in pleasure like I'd never experienced.

36

Stell

"I'M NOT GOING BACK to Philly with you."

Vaughn gave me his usual smug smile. He had no conception of being turned down. It just hadn't occurred to him that it could ever happen.

What a way to go through life. Maybe it was an advantage, to always assume things were going to work out in your favor. On the other hand, when they didn't, it must be fucking devastating.

And Vaughn was about to find out what that felt like.

He stood casually leaning against the outside wall of Tableau, where he'd insisted on meeting me. I'd tried to convince him they would never let him in, but he thought if we were back together, there was no way they could lock him out.

Wrong.

"Okay, Stell," he said in a grindingly patronizing tone, "whatever you say."

Damn. He had the nerve to mock me.

That's when Maze, Robbie, and Cab came out the door and headed our way.

Vaughn's eyes grew wide and his arms dropped to his sides. He wasn't expecting company.

But he held his chin up. "What the hell do you guys want? Are these your henchmen?" he asked, looking at me and laughing.

"Vaughn, I told you I'm not going back to Philly with you. In fact, I'm not going anywhere with you. You make me sick. My friends are here to make sure you understand that, loud and clear."

"Bullshit," he said, rolling his eyes. "Stell, I know you don't want that picture of your whoring around to come out when your dad is in a tight reelection race."

Such. A. Fucker.

"Do what you have to do, Vaughn, I'm going inside to work. The guys here will be having a little conversation with you."

Anger flashed across his face. "What the hell? I'm not talking to these losers. I'm talking to you."

Maze, Robbie, and Cab walked toward him, with the bouncers watching closely in the background.

"You're not talking to her anymore, pal," Robbie said.

Just before I let the door swing shut behind me, I looked over my shoulder at what I hoped would be the last time I ever laid eyes on Vaughn Breslin. The guys formed a circle around him and when he took a swing at Maze, Cab caught his arm and twisted it behind his back. He screamed like a baby.

I didn't need to see any more. But I had a feeling that when they were done with him, he'd be heading back to Philly, fast.

I called my parents from the office, even though it was late on the East Coast.

"Mom. Is Dad there? I'd like to talk to you both."

I heard her rustling around the kitchen. "Yes, he's here, dear. He doesn't head back to DC until tomorrow morning. *Honey*!" she called.

They pressed the speaker button, and we were all connected.

"Hey, Dad."

"Hello, Estella. What's going on that you asked us to both be on the phone?"

I took a deep breath. This wasn't going to be pretty.

"Vaughn came to Denver to try and convince me to return to Philly with him. When I said no, he got a photo of me… dancing. You see, I took a part-time job at a nightclub."

"Oh, honey, you're not waitressing, are you?" Mom asked.

"No, Mom. I help the bartenders when it's busy."

I could see her looking at my dad, her eyes wide. "Oh. Well, that sounds like fun."

If she only knew.

"So he got an unflattering picture of me having fun, and tried to bribe me with it, saying if I didn't come back with him, he'd give it to the press to make your reelection difficult."

I could picture my father with his pissed-off face. Which would be getting more pissed off by the moment.

"Well. That's extortion," he huffed. "But what is it about the picture that makes him think it will cause trouble for the campaign?"

I smiled at his indignation. Politicians were good at that shit.

And how bad could the photo be? I'd never seen it.

At least he hadn't gotten a photo of when I'd stripped for the guys on the platform. Now that would be a real problem.

"I don't know, Dad. I was having fun. Nothing outrageous."

Fingers crossed.

"That's just terrible, dear. What did you tell him?" Mom asked.

"I told him to take a hike."

My father burst out laughing.

I did *not* expect that.

"That's perfect, honey. Never give in to someone who operates that way. I'm proud of you."

What? Had I heard that right?

"I… thought you guys wanted me to marry him. You're not mad?"

"Oh, honey, we thought *you* wanted to marry him, and we were trying to help," Mom said.

"Stell, he's a sniveling bootlicker. I never liked him," Dad boomed.

Huh?

Were a thousand pounds just lifted from my shoulders? Because it sure felt like it.

"You're not mad that he's taking the photo to the press?" I asked, incredulous.

My dad sighed. "Do you have your clothes on in it?"

I laughed. "Of course."

"Well then, there is nothing to worry about. You're a grown woman, and you have a life."

Wow. Basically what Marni had said.

Damn. Sometimes people really do surprise you.

37

Stell

THE GUYS FILTERED into the office as I finished with Mom and Dad.

"Well, you won't be seeing any more of him," Robbie said, clapping his hands together like he'd just washed something dirty off them.

I grimaced. I couldn't help it. "What… what did you do to him?"

I was actually terrified to ask, but I also wanted reassurance he was gone.

The guys looked at each other.

Maze shrugged. "We had a talk with him, and then had the bouncers emphasize our point."

What the hell did that mean?

Never mind, I didn't want to know.

"So, you think he's gone, like forever? And that he's going to leave me alone?" I asked hopefully.

"If he doesn't, he's a glutton for punishment. Our security guys—I mean, bouncers—know a lot of people."

Um, okay. That's all I needed to know.

A lump grew in my throat, and I knew what was coming. I really didn't want to get emotional with the guys, especially at the club.

But I did anyway.

My bottom lip quivered, and a couple tears ran down my cheeks. "I'm sorry. I didn't mean to act like this. But I'm so grateful. To all of you. You've been kind in so many ways. It's been so unexpected."

Maze came over and hooked a finger under my chin to meet my gaze. "You know what's unexpected? *You*." He wiped the tears off my cheeks with his thumb, then tasted them.

"See?" I said, choking on my words. "You do things like that and I… don't even know what to say."

I also didn't know what to feel, my insides broiling with a hundred emotions, hampering my ability to think straight.

"I know what you can say, darlin'," Robbie said.

We looked at him.

He walked over, and taking one of my hands, kissed the back of it. "Tell us you'll stay. That you'll stay here in Denver. With us."

Well, shit. Now the tears really began to fall. I couldn't speak.

So I just nodded.

Cab laughed. "And... what does that mean?"

"It means… that… I say yes," I managed to blurt.

His face broke into the biggest smile I'd ever seen on him and he turned to the guys, who he started high-fiving. Then, he wrapped his arms around me and twirled me the best he could in the confines of the small office. By the time he set me down, my tears had dried and I was actually laughing.

He ran to the office door and locked it.

"Don't you guys have to get to work in a bit?" I asked. "I have to get over to my yoga class."

"We have a few minutes," he said, backing me up to the desk.

Behind me, Robbie pushed aside a pile of papers and other junk, and Cab laid me back.

Maze pulled my booties and socks off while Robbie shimmied my jeans down. As soon as they were dangling from one foot, he pushed my knees apart, exposing my most private parts.

But instead of feeling shy or embarrassed, I reveled in their admiring eyes. They liked me, thought I was sexy, smart, and beautiful, and being vulnerable with them made us that much closer.

"Mmmm," Robbie said, running a finger up my wet slit and tasting it. "Guys, each of you take one leg while I go to town on our girl here."

Holy crap.

Maze got on one side of me and Cab, the other. With my back on the desk, and my butt nearly hanging off its edge, they pushed my knees back to open me further while Robbie buried his face in my pussy.

I raised my hands over my head to brace myself against the wall behind the desk, and arched in response to the sweet sensation of being lapped from ass to clit. Little explosions of pleasure detonated all over my body, and my breath came in gasps, a sure sign that release was around the corner.

"Whew, look at Robbie go. Leave some for us, dude."

I burst out laughing. Couldn't help it.

Robbie circled my clit with his tongue while entering me with two fingers. As he increased his suction on my hard bud, he pumped my pussy faster.

"Oh god," I cried. "I'm coming."

My entire body began to buck, and it was a good thing Maze and Cab were holding me. The orgasm hit me like a truck, leaving me tossing my head from side to side and pounding my fists on the desk underneath me.

"Oh my god. Oh my god, you guys," I breathed.

Robbie leaned up between my spread legs and over my still-shaking body to kiss me.

"Mmmm," he said, "I wanted to share that taste with you."

"I… it… oh shit… I can't seem to speak," I said, laughing.

"Have you had enough, baby? Because I think Maze has plans for you," he said.

We all looked in Maze's direction, where he'd dropped his jeans. His hard dick was covered with a condom and he was heading my way.

"Well, aren't you a little sneak?" I laughed.

With his perfect, thick, cock bouncing, he raised his hands like he was under arrest. "Guilty as charged, ma'am."

"Well, at least you didn't wreck my car. Like some people here."

Robbie rolled his eyes.

"But you can wreck my pussy," I offered, rubbing between my legs and opening myself just enough to tempt him.

"Jesus. Are you trying to fucking kill me?" Maze asked, positioning himself where I could direct his cock.

"If she kills you, at least you'll die happy," Cab said.

"You ready?"

I nodded. "I think so. Try not to hurt me, big man."

He closed his eyes, and shaking his head at all the silliness, pushed into me.

Fuck. I gasped as I adjusted to the slow movement of his hips, just enough to shoot chills all over my body, as if he wanted to relish our connection and make it last forever.

Hands wandered over my body. I didn't even know how many. Someone had pulled my T-shirt up and pushed my bra down to play with my tits, and another alternated between kissing my lips, temples, and neck.

With my eyes closed, I had no idea who was doing what. I didn't care. Never had so many sensations plowed through me at one time.

When I finally looked, I saw the veins in Maze's forehead bulge. He thrust hard and deep until his balls bounced against me, bellowing loudly enough for the entire club to hear. And when he pumped me a last few times, I exploded in yet another orgasm that left me unable to think or speak.

I was breathing like I'd run a sprint. Wrecked. Absolutely wrecked.

Robbie whispered in my ear. "Did you like that darlin'?"

"Oh god yeah," I groaned.

I was amazed. Amazed that I was right where I wanted to be without even looking for it. Funny how things fall into your lap.

I shook my head to get the fuzz out as the guys dressed me. "I want more. But I have to get to yoga."

Robbie popped a kiss on my lips. "We want more, too, darlin'. This is just the beginning."

38

Maze

"You make a good babysitter."

Stell rubbed Jax's mostly-bald little head, which protruded from the baby pack on her chest.

She gestured toward the door. "Robbie's right behind us with Jax's stuff. I thought it might be fun to hold him. Until he poops or starts crying, that is."

"Hey, guys," Robbie said, sweating and bustling in with what seemed like a week's worth of luggage.

Both Stell and I looked at him, skeptical that a tiny human needed all that.

He held his hands up. "I know it looks like a lot of stuff. But it pays to be prepared."

"A lot of stuff? It looks like you're dropping him off at college," I said.

He considered all his bags. "Could be overkill. What can I say? I'm still perfecting my dad technique."

In his sleep, Jax gave a little snort and smacked his lips. Stell put her hand over her mouth to keep from laughing.

"What's up with the custody thing?" I asked.

"Hey, guys, sorry I'm late," Cab called, blowing in the door and rushing right over to lay a juicy kiss on our girl.

Robbie took a deep breath and shook his head. "Oh, man. Crazy shit. Elise is in jail, if you can believe it. I guess she and an old boyfriend were selling drugs or something. I don't know how everything will pan out, but for now the little guy is all mine. And to think she wanted to leave town with him, Jesus. Her mother's money will get her out of trouble, but I'm making the case for full custody."

He picked up Jax's foot from where it dangled against Stell's chest and kissed it.

Who knew Robbie would make such an awesome dad?

He'd knocked up the wrong girl, but look what came of it.

"Speaking of dads," Cab said, "I actually had a somewhat positive conversation with my father this morning. He complimented our business acumen in closing Tableau and opening a new place."

Wonders never ceased.

It was going to feel good to start over with a different concept. We'd sold Tableau for a very nice price and paid back Cab's father. We were now opening a members-only club with cozy seating areas, a full kitchen, a few hotel rooms on the top floor, meeting spaces, and a gym.

That's right. Marni was moving Altitude to our new place.

Which was as of yet, unnamed.

Stell had suggested License & Registration, which apparently were the first words she'd heard spoken when she arrived in Denver, thanks to Robbie smashing into her car.

But she was only kidding. At least I hoped so. Clever idea, but no go.

Our beautiful Stell. I felt like I'd won the damn lottery.

And so did the other guys.

We were beyond psyched that she was staying. And she was not only staying, but she was staying for *us*.

So fucking awesome.

We walked around the old, abandoned candy factory that was to be our new club. It was massive, which was how we were able to do so much with it. We'd repaid my dad and gotten real investors this time, not the kind who would arbitrarily pull the plug. It was all going to be fucking amazing.

"Would you look at this place," Cab said, kicking up

dust and dirt as he wandered through the dimly lit building.

Although pretty much trashed at the moment, the place had a magical level of potential with its old-school casement windows, sky-high ceilings, and exposed beams and ironwork.

"This is going to be amazing," Stell agreed. "I can lead my yoga classes on the roof when it's nice out."

"Hey, congrats to your dad on his reelection," Cab said.

"Eh. He was probably always going to win. Despite Vaughn's efforts to sabotage him," Stell said.

Vaughn had well and truly shot himself in the foot. Not only had his actions not had one iota of impact on Congressman Kline's campaign, but he'd also made an enemy for life out of the man.

Vaughn turned out to be a dummy. But we knew any man who would stray from Stell had to be an idiot.

I looked around at the cavernous room and could imagine people meeting friends for a mellow lunch or dinner, having parties and celebrations, and coming in for their regular Altitude workouts. The wild, loud, dance-filled nightclub was something we'd grown out of. It was fun for a while. But we were ready for something a little more adult now.

But not too adult.

We'd still be bartenders. And most importantly, Stell would still be our girl.

There were lots of unknowns about what lay ahead,

but with the beautiful little family we'd put together, we were confident we could handle anything that came our way.

Did you like *Her Dirty Bartenders*? Learn about the next book in the Men at Work series,
Her Dirty Ranchers

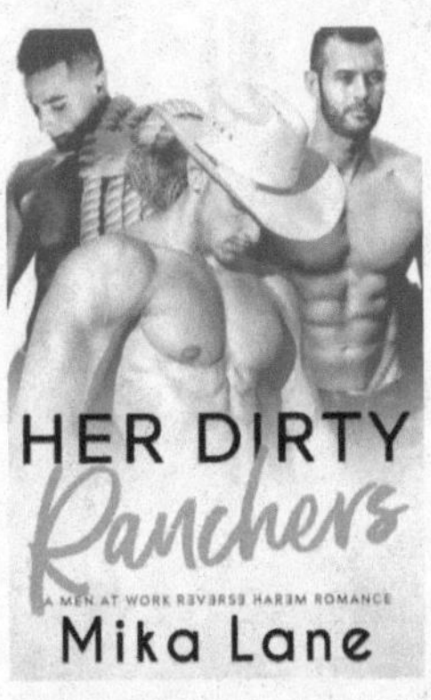

I hope you loved reading this book as much as I loved writing it. Please visit my store to learn more about my books, and to buy directly from me!
https://mikalaneshop.com/

SHOP
Mika
Lane

ABOUT THE AUTHOR

Dear Reader:

I'm USA TODAY bestselling romance author Mika Lane, and am OBSESSED with bringing you sassy, steamy stories with imperfect heroines and the bad-a*s dudes they bring to their knees. I'll always bring you my signature humor and heat, topped off with a modern-day happily ever after.

My first book ever was *The Day I Ate the Milkyway*, a true fourth-grade masterpiece illustrated with crayons and bound with construction paper and glue. Nowadays, steamy romance gives purpose to my days and nights as I create worlds and characters that tickle the imagination. I live in magical Northern California with my own handsome alpha dude, sometimes known as Mr. Mika Lane, and two devilish cats named Chuck and Murray.

A dual citizen of the United States and Ireland, I have on more than one occasion spent my last dollar on a plane ticket somewhere, and am always planning my next escape. I often try new recipes on unsuspecting friends, search out hiding places to read undisturbed, and sadly kill every houseplant I bring home.

I LOVE to hear from readers when I'm not dreaming up naughty tales to share. Visit my online shop https:// mikalaneshop.com/ and say hello https:// mikalaneshop.com/pages/meet-mika.

xoxo, Mika

www.ingramcontent.com/pod-product-compliance
Lightning Source LLC
Chambersburg PA
CBHW010345170726
48284CB00009B/2799